CN00865044

The Willow Cottage Series:

Christmas Wishes

At

Willow Cottage

by
CLARE CASSY

In memory of Enid
who really did sing at Raffles Hotel.

Thank you to Martin for his unstinting patience and support.
My super-talented hero.

Cover design and layout: illuminati-design.co.uk

The Willow Cottage Series:

Christmas Wishes At Willow Cottage

By

CLARE CASSY

Milly

Milly sighed as she fixed the butterfly clasps on her pearl earrings. *Don't cry, don't you dare cry, she admonished herself as she checked her make-up in her bedroom mirror. Your guests are relying on you to create a wonderful Christmas. Put on that smile and dazzle them with your turkey…*

This was Milly's first Christmas without her beloved husband Bill.

This time last year they were opening their Christmas stockings while enjoying a cup of tea from the Teasmade on their bedside table. Silly really, two people in their seventies having a Christmas stocking. But that's what they did, each and every year that they were married. They even got one for their dog Rufus - a special dog one of course, with chews and other dog treats. Just the three of them in this room laughing at what Santa brought them before they went downstairs to enjoy the rest of the day with their extended families - Bill wearing his Christmas jumper and Milly, those silly reindeer ears. Well, one did it for the grandchildren. With sixteen bedrooms, it always made sense for everyone to come to 'Willow Cottage'. But things were different this year. Milly had never imagined spending a Christmas without Bill, but that was life wasn't it? One of you had to go first.

So, she'd be serving twelve assorted guests who'd all booked in specially for the holiday, Christmas brunch at midday followed by dinner at seven. But oh, how her heart ached for Bill, bossing her about, directing proceedings in the kitchen. Milly's eyes watered at the memories but no, she had to keep a lid on things. Plenty of time to weep into her pillow later. One more quick dab of face powder and she should made her way downstairs to fix a special Christmas breakfast for Flora, the permanent resident she inherited when she moved into 'Willow Cottage'.

Of course, the family were concerned. They didn't want her in 'Willow Cottage' on her own at Christmas, albeit with twelve guests. They urged her to post the 'No Vacancy' sign on her door, shut up her B&B business for the Christmas break, leave 'Willow Cottage' and spend Christmas with them. But in all truth, Milly wasn't in the frame of mind to celebrate without Bill, it didn't seem right and would just be too painful. Besides, her daughter Sophie, was a backing singer and had the opportunity to go on a Christmas tour with one of those well-known boy bands - Milly couldn't recall which one. Her daughter had to shelve her singing career when she had Hope; life as a touring musician and single-parent with a small child just didn't work, but now that Hope had turned twenty-one and had been invited to spend Christmas with her boyfriend's family, she was the first one to insist that her mother should seize this chance and go back on tour.

Milly's two boys, Jake and Cy were in America with their respective wives and children. Zac, her unofficial grandson, was backpacking in New Zealand while Bill's son Charlie, was spending Christmas with his girlfriend's parents.

No, Milly had to face her newfound singledom this Christmas and in all truth, she was happier looking after other, she suspected, lost and lonely people like her, in the comfort and security of 'Willow Cottage'.

That young couple in the 'Wallflower Room' - what or whom were they escaping from? One would have thought they would prefer to spend their Christmas abroad in the sun. But with all the current travel restrictions they'd probably decided against it.

The charming old lady and her son - most probably she had been recently widowed. How nice of him to bring her back to 'Willow Cottage'. He'd told Milly about the holidays they used to spend at the house when he was a child. Apparently, a Mrs and Mrs Hollis were the owners then...

Then there was Gwen Cartwright, the author who had been staying at 'Willow Cottage' on a regular basis for more years than Milly had been in the house. She too also remembered several of the previous owners and always stayed in the 'Heliotrope Room,' right at the top of the house. It was in that room that she had the inspiration to write *The Honey Pot Years* - one of her most famous novels.

A single lady of an indeterminate age, she had no immediate family and never liked to intrude on friends' family Christmases.

Milly didn't know anything about the elderly gentleman in the 'Foxglove' room, or the young man in the 'Gardenia' but they seemed friendly enough.

And of course, she had her charming Afghan family, Nazim and Moola and their two children, Ten-year-old Maryam and eighteen-month-old Karim. They'd fled the carnage in Kabul just over three months ago and were lodging with her in the Brewery - an adjoining, more self-contained annex to the house, until they could be housed more permanently.

Of course, they were Muslim and didn't celebrate Christmas but they were so keen to embrace their new lives in the UK, Milly couldn't resist buying a Christmas gift for the children.

It's Christmas morning and I'm going to pop in their present now. Sorry, Flora my darling, you are going to have to wait a bit for your breakfast.

Her arms laden with the brightly wrapped parcels, Milly knocked on the door to the family's room.

"Good Morning Moola, Merry Christmas. I hope this isn't too early but I just wanted to pop a few presents in for the children before I get Flora's breakfast."

It clearly was, because Moola didn't have her hair covered and the children weren't dressed. Milly wouldn't normally knock so early but she knew the day would run away with itself.

"Merry Christmas Mrs Milly and Salaam Alaikum, as we say in my country."

"Salaam Alaikum." Milly responded much to Moola's delight. She understood this meant 'Peace be with you.'

Moola spoke very good English. Her husband Nazim had been an interpreter for the British army and he had taught her and their children English at home. She spoke in her own language to the children who rushed over to the door.

"Merry Christmas Maryam, Salaam Alaikum," Milly said, bending down to give her gift - a beautifully adorned doll called Anna from the Disney film, *Frozen*. Clutching the present to her chest, the little girl looked totally overcome.

"And Merry Christmas Karim, Salaam Alaikum," Milly added, giving the beautiful eighteen-month boy with his huge brown eyes and mop of black curls, a brightly wrapped Thomas the Tank Engine train. Moola's eyes filled with tears.

"This is so kind of you Mrs Milly, we thank you with all my heart."

Moola spoke to Maryam in her own language, encouraging the child to repeat after her in English:

"Thank you Mrs Milly."

"Thank you Mrs Milly." the child repeated, shyly.

"For my beautiful present."

"For my beautiful present."

Embarrassed, Maryam nestled closer to her mother still tightly clutching her precious doll to her chest.

"You speak very good English Maryam," Milly smiled, she was such a lovely little girl with her huge, round, saucer shaped dark eyes. "I hope you are going to come down to dinner tonight with your Mummy and Daddy so I can show you my special Christmas tree?" The little girl looked askance at her mother.

"That is very kind Mrs Milly but we don't want to put you to any trouble."

"It's no trouble Moola, Christmas dinner is my gift to you. This is your first Christmas in England and I want it to be special. Besides Christmas isn't Christmas without children."

They had got to know each other a little. Moola had run her own beauty salon in Kabul which she had to close when the Taliban took over. As quite a well-known make-up artist, she had to go into hiding along with her husband, as the Taliban strongly disapproved of women using make-up. Her shop front had been defaced and for the safety of herself, her staff and customers, she had to close the business. The whole story came out, when Milly asked her to update her makeup one evening. They'd had such fun that night and Milly noticed what a great hands-on father and husband Nazim was - encouraging his wife to go downstairs with Milly while he looked after the children.

"Now, Mrs Milly, do you wear blusher?" Moola had asked, holding up her palette of makeup.

"No dear, I've never got on with it. I can't seem to put it on properly."

"You should always wear blusher," she tutted. "Now do this," she said smiling, "And see here?" she pointed to the apples of her own beautiful cheeks, "This is where you put the blusher... just like this." She flicked her fat brush. Of course she looked effortlessly gorgeous. "You try," she said passing over the palette and brush.
Milly stretched her face into a smile and did as directed under Moola's watchful eye.

"Beautiful - there you go, look at yourself," she said flashing her mirror "You can do it Mrs Milly!"

"Ooh yes, that does look good." No one was more surprised than Milly. "I hope I can remember to do it like this next time."

"You will, Mrs Milly, it's just practice, just remember to smile and put the colour just... here..."
Moola had even persuaded Milly to change the colour of her usual lipstick from a darkish red to lighter pink along with some lip-liner to make her lips look a little fuller. And, Milly had to concede that she immediately looked ten years younger.

"I hope you will be wearing your blusher tonight," Moola joked as Milly turned to walk back into the main part of the house.

"Most definitely Moola, it is Christmas!"

"Thank you so much Mrs Milly," she called after her retreating figure, "Thank you for everything, I think we are going to like your English Christmas."

**

Flora

Flora sat in her usual spot by the window, waiting for Milly. Her room was her world and she rarely ventured out of it, although if the weather was nice she could be encouraged to sit in the garden under the old fig tree. She liked sitting by her window, watching the world go by, people crossing the road to go into the Post Office. People walking down to the duck pond past the Bull's Head pub with their dogs tugging on leads. Parents with little children, scuffing their feet or running ahead. Sometimes the parents got cross if they didn't hold their hand. Flora had seen it all.

She'd been to the duck pond with Milly a few times. They'd fed the ducks and ate cheese and pickle sandwiches on the little wooden seat under the Weeping Willow tree but it was never long before Flora got fidgety, making it very obvious that she wished to return to the safety of her room. She liked her room with its candy box pink, striped wallpaper.

She had a white, kidney-shaped, dressing table with a glass top and pink skirt of curtains which covered the drawers. The silver brush and comb set, engraved with her initials when she was a child, looked so pretty displayed alongside the big pink fluffy powder puff Milly had given her for one of her birthdays. Of course she never used it, it was far too special. She had her own television set and Milly would sometimes put on a programme about wildlife for her. But she didn't watch it much, preferring to sit in the quiet, comforting, solitude of her room. This worried Milly. The only real social interaction Flora had was when she went to the Day Centre in Chichester, but this had now been closed and so Flora's world was shrinking by the day. Milly tried her best, and made it a point to ask her down for coffee in the dining room with her every Wednesday. But as Flora retreated further into her world over her coffee cup, Milly suspected that even these weekly chats were as stressful for Flora as they were for her.

But, hey ho, it was Christmas Day and Milly would insist she came downstairs to see the Christmas tree and unwrap her present in the dining room with her.

The birds were chirping and hopping about on the branches of the cherry tree outside Flora's window. They always flew down when Milly filled the bird feeder in the front garden. Flora liked the birds. Milly said they were sparrows. After her usual, polite knock on the door, Milly stepped into Flora's room.

"Good morning dear, Merry Christmas."

"Is it Christmas?" Flora looked confused.

"Yes, it certainly is. All day, and I have brought you a special breakfast."

Milly placed Flora's special tray on her lap. Decorated with a mini Christmas tree and sprig of holly, there were a couple of smoked salmon canapes, glass of fizzy apple juice, a croissant and little dish of marmalade alongside her usual small pot of tea.

"Thank you Milly," Flora said in her small voice, her papery fingers pinching the tiny baubles on the little tree.

"Now, what are you going to wear today Flora? Something special as it is Christmas Day I hope."

Milly opened Flora's wardrobe door and looked inside, selecting a pretty, blue floral dress which she held up for Flora's approval. Flora eyed the dress thoughtfully.

"Do you know Milly, I had seven dance frocks when I was a girl growing up in Singapore, seven dance frocks… All specially made for me, every year, in the finest silk."

Milly had heard the story of Flora's dance frocks many times but was always adept at pretending she hadn't.

"Yes, I had seven dance frocks," she repeated, looking into the distance as she related the story. "I was just sixteen years old you know when I sang to all the army officers in 'Raffles Hotel'. They were all dressed in their finest clothes. My father, mother and sisters were all there. He was a diplomat and wore a white suit with a scarlet sash around his waist. My mother wore her traditional,

Malaysian sarong kebaya, her black hair piled high on her head with a white Gardenia tucked behind her ear.
She looked so beautiful." Flora looked wistful, staring into the distance for a private moment. "I can always remember the song I sang... It was *When the lights go on again* by Eddie Seiler. There were so many people there, I thought I would be sick but I just looked at my mother and sang to her…"

"It must have been a wonderful childhood Flora, growing up in Singapore."

"It was, I had four sisters you know? Constance, Cora, Emily and June. I was the eldest. Our family had servants but my mother always used to say the other diplomats' wives used to look down on her," she lowered her voice, theatrically, "Because Father had married 'a Malay'." Flora took a bite of her canapé. "See that picture over there Milly? That was my husband - 'handsome is as handsome does'," she added in a dark tone.
Milly glanced over at the good looking, albeit shifty looking young lad in his military uniform.

"I should never have married him. We eloped you know? My family cut me off… never heard from them again. I wrote letters but they never answered. Not even my mother or my favourite sister, June. My father forbid them to write to me."

"That is so sad Flora, I am very sorry. You never heard what happened to your sisters? Did they all marry?"
Flora shook her head. She never knew what became of them. Milly knew the sad story. Flora had been spirited away to England by a young squaddie stationed in Malaysia. This was how she ended up in Chichester. When they eloped, he brought her back to the family home with disastrous consequences. She was never accepted by them.

"His mother said she didn't like my crinkly hair and said my skin looked dirty." Flora had told Milly on one occasion. Things went from bad to worse. "I couldn't believe they lived in such a small, pokey house and didn't have one servant. All his mother did was clean all day."

Worlds apart, Flora's husband was clearly ashamed of her and confined her to the house. Growing up in a family who had servants, Flora had no idea of domestic management and when her husband died some years later, she had a mental breakdown. She couldn't cope on her own, had never been to the shops or cleaned a house. She simply didn't know how. Once her circumstances came to light, Social Services placed her in residential care at 'Willow Cottage'. Milly didn't have the heart to turn her out when she bought the house. This inoffensive lady who was terrified of her own shadow and occupied just one room - how could she? Besides, 'Willow Cottage' was being sold as an 'up and running' B&B business, so Flora was really a permanent, paying guest. And one Milly was to grow very fond of.

"So are you going to come down for your Christmas dinner a bit later? And get your present from the Christmas tree Flora?" Milly asked hopefully, "It is Christmas and I would like you to see all the decorations. So, once you have put on your pretty dress you can come down, I've got a couple of crackers for us to pull."

***

The turkey and all the trimmings were roasting nicely in the aga and Milly's guests had all revelled in the culinary delights of their special Christmas brunch. Smoked salmon blinis with a spoonful of sour cream and delicate topping of lump fish roe - a very convincing fake caviar. One of Bill's specials - it never failed to impress.

It was getting on for one o'clock, time for Milly and Flora to have their Christmas lunch together in the dining room. There was no way in the world that Flora would want to come down and join the other guests; it made sense for the two of them to eat together so Milly had prepared their Christmas lunch separately.

"Ready Flora?" She asked as she entered her room. Flora was standing in the middle of her room in her pretty blue dress, looking awkward and self-conscious.

"Oh, you look so pretty, I love you in that dress."

"Thank you Milly," she answered, looking overcome.

"You look very pretty too." She added graciously.
They walked down the stairs, Milly watching Flora like a
mother hen. She looked even tinier and more frail out of
the confines of her world. Gripping on to the bannisters,
Flora slowly made her way down the stairs politely
commentating on the silvery streamers and clusters of
holly hanging from the lights and pictures in the hall,
before walking nervously into the dining room.

"It's just the two of us," Milly reassured her.
Flora looked hugely relieved then clapped her hands
together like a little child when she saw the towering
Christmas tree festooned with hundreds of sparkling fairy
lights. Milly beckoned her towards it.

"Go on, pick a chocolate," Milly encouraged her, "I
will allow you to eat one now if you promise to eat your
dinner."
Flora's tiny wizened hand reached towards the tree and
plucked a chocolate Father Christmas from a branch.

"Here are our presents from Santa," Milly joked,
bending down under the tree to retrieve them. "One for
you and one for me."
Then directing her towards their table they opened their
presents. Flora slowly and very carefully unfurled the
silver, embossed wrapping paper to reveal a pretty blue
cardigan and sparkly hair clip.

"Now, when we next see Sophie, she will do your
hair for you Flora. Remember how you liked your hair
when she put it up for you that time?"

"Yes, I do, thank you Milly."

"That cardigan is the perfect colour to go with that
dress," Milly assured her.

"It is," Flora acquiesced politely.
Milly proceeded to open her gift.

"Ooh" she gushed, "Some Nina Ricci perfume, my
favourite. Now let's pull a cracker and maybe play a little
game before we eat."

They both put on their paper hats. Flora's was far too big and kept slipping down over her eyes.

Milly read the jokes.

"What does Santa suffer from if he gets stuck in a chimney?"

Flora's face was deadpan.

"Claus-trophobia!"

Milly passed her the next joke. Flora read it laboriously in a flat, expressionless tone.

"What happens to elves when they are naughty?"

"I have no idea Flora, what happens to elves when they are naughty?"

"Santa gives them the sack…"

"Oh that is funny," Milly laughed.

Again, there was no response from Flora.

Milly proceeded to set up a game of Snakes and Ladders which was marginally more successful although Flora got a little confused about when to go up the ladders or down the snakes. Milly had a much-needed glass of sherry, Flora a glass of fizzy apple juice and they finished the game.

"Merry Christmas Flora," she said clinking her glass.

"Merry Christmas Milly."

Flora, as usual, ate like a little bird. Milly had voiced her concerns to Flora's social worker as she never seemed to take any interest in food. Not even cake.

"I do worry about her sitting up there in her room all day," she added, "She just stares out of the window. I'm the only person she talks to and that's no more than a couple of words each day…"

"You do a great job Mrs Henderson." Jennie Bird, Flora's social worker assured her. "It was very good of you to keep Flora on when you bought the house. We didn't think you would."

"I couldn't turn her out after this has been her home for so many years and it's not as if I am not paid quite well to look after her. It's just, I do worry, the visits to the Day Centre were good for her. These wretched cutbacks…"

"I know," Jennie Bird sighed. "Do you think she could benefit from joining a small choir for people with

dementia and other special needs? The conductor is very experienced in working with these people. They put on the odd concert and meet every week in Fishbourne church hall for a good old sing-song and have coffee and biscuits afterwards. Transport is laid on..."
Milly thought for a moment.

"Yes, she may like that, she sang when she was young and tells a lovely story about standing up and singing in the famous 'Raffles Hotel' when she was a teen-ager. Her father was a diplomat."

"My goodness," Jennie Bird responded. "Who'd have thought it? Our little Flora..."

To Milly's surprise and delight. Flora agreed to go. Milly accompanied her to the first session. They were a bit of a motley crew. A few people from Chichester's homeless shelter were there, dozing in the corner along with a couple of people with dementia and their carers, and then there was Flora. Mathew, their friendly conductor, chivvied them into a semi-circle.

"Right now everyone - let's start with a few scales, shall we? Doh, Ray, Me, Far, So, La, Ti, Doh... Repeat after me..."
The carers appeared to be a lot more enthusiastic than everyone else. Flora sang along in her head not yet ready to find her voice. Mathew persevered enthusiastically. The first song they sang was *If you don't know me by now* by Simply Red. This was to be their song for the next couple of weeks. Flora liked it, again singing along in her head and tapping her toes to the music. The fourth week she went, everyone was familiar with the lyrics and Mathew asked if anyone wanted to stand up and sing it solo. Biddy, an elderly lady in her eighties, bravely had a go. What she lacked in musical ability she more than made up for with enthusiasm. It was excruciating, even the carers winced but you would never have known it from anyone's face except Flora's. Mathew was just delighted that some-one had the courage to stand up and sing and beamed encouragingly throughout her performance.

Flora wrestled with herself.

I sang in Raffles Hotel, to all those officers, when I was just sixteen. I can jolly well show her how to sing!
So once Biddy had finished, Flora gingerly raised her hand.

"Flora, how lovely, ready?" Mathew warmly encouraged her as all the carers clapped.
Flora felt a flurry of nerves but pictured her mother's face and sang to her, and to her only.

If you don't know me by now
You will never, never, never know me
Oooh
Now all the things that we've been through
You should understand me
Like I understand you…

A hush fell over the room. She had perfect pitch and no one was more astounded than Mathew. Everyone burst into applause as she finished her song. Mathew and all the carers were quite overcome. A few had tears in their eyes. This shy old lady who never said boo to a goose, who would have thought it? She was sensational.

Flora eagerly anticipated her weekly meetings with Mathew and the choir. When their Christmas concert had been cancelled, after weeks of rehearsals, Flora was distraught, she had so wanted Milly to be there and was going to surprise her with her solo. Mathew, sensing her disappointment slipped something into her hand as they were all leaving after their last session before the Christmas break.

"Flora, this is a recording of you singing. We know how much you wanted Milly to come to the concert so this is the next best thing."
Flora's eyes filled with tears.

"Now you will be back in the new year won't you Flora? You are my star performer you know…" he whispered conspiratorially.

"So, Flora, do you have any Christmas wishes?" Milly asked as they finished their Christmas pudding. Flora lowered her eyes and tried to search for the appropriate words as she fished in the pocket of her dress for a small, clumsily wrapped package which she carefully placed on the table between them. Luckily, she always kept the wrapping paper from any presents she was given.

"Oh goodness, thank you Flora this is a surprise," Milly said picking it up. It had been customary for Milly to buy her own gift from her each Christmas because Flora never went shopping - the hustle and bustle of crowds was too overwhelming at the best of times, let alone Christmas. When Milly peeled off the wrapping she saw it was a CD with the words 'Flora's solo' written on it in black marker pen.

"Oh my goodness Flora, is this what I think it is?" Milly leapt up from the dining table and taking Flora by her hand they went into Milly's part of the house where she directed Flora to sit down on the sofa. In all the years that Flora had lived in the house she had never been into Milly's private sitting room. Her eyes were immediately drawn to the piano. A beautiful baby grand in the corner of the room. It had belonged to Milly's mother, who was a keen pianist. As if drawn by a magnet Flora made her way over to it, stroking the top lovingly with her fingers she edged towards the piano stool.

"Do you play the piano Flora?" Milly asked, stopping in front of the CD player.

"I did when I was a girl."

"Sit down, I would love to hear you play something. Would you like some sheet music?"
Flora shook her head. Sat down at the piano and stared at the keys, lost in a world of her own. Then, all of a sudden, her tiny papery fingers touched the keys. Cautiously she played a few notes. Milly was spellbound. Then her fingers took over and the room was filled with the most melodic piano playing. It was as if her hands weren't hers.

In all the years she had looked after Flora, Milly hadn't known she could play the piano. *I'm so ashamed. This beautiful instrument sitting here untouched all this time and Flora, such a wonderful pianist.* Now she knew what they would do on those interminable coffee mornings. She would simply bring Flora in here to play the piano.

As Flora finished her piece, Milly was aware she still had her CD in her hand. Putting it into her CD, she adjusted the volume and the room resounded with the sweetest, most angelic voice singing '*I'm dreaming of a white Christmas,*' Milly's eyes filled with tears as she took Flora's hand in her own.

"Flora, this is quite, quite marvellous. Thank you, so much." Milly got up from the sofa and played the tape again.

For the first time in her life, Flora's dearest wish had come true. Her beloved Milly could hear her sing. And she got to play the piano again too.

***

Hester

There it was, Julian's family home. 'Chestnut House.' An imposing Victorian pile set back off the road. Hester quickly parked around the corner from the house. She'd borrowed her sister's zippy little, banana yellow, Mini Clubman as she couldn't possibly turn up in her old battered Skoda. Her heart was racing and she felt breathless. Her hands gripped the steering wheel. Counting to ten as she took three long breaths, she checked her hair and make-up in the car mirror.

You've done it again haven't you Hester Wright? She admonished herself out loud as she spruced up her complexion with a quick flick of blusher.

You knew you didn't really want to do this. You just couldn't say no, could you?

'But Hester dear, you've only known this young man a couple of weeks, do you really want to spend Christmas day with a family you haven't even met?' Her mother had tried to reason with her but Hester had been swept off her feet. If this incredible, blonde Adonis wanted her to spend Christmas with him and his family, nothing and no one would stop her. But that was then and this was now. Checking her watch she saw that she was an hour late already. Another deep breath and she would open the car door, retrieve the tastefully wrapped gifts for Julian and his family from the boot and make her entrance.

I can't do it. I just can't get out of the car…

Overwhelmed by an awful urge to escape, she put the car into gear and drove on, her heart racing. It wasn't long before she spotted a large black and white, wrought iron sign-post, leading into a 'Willow Cottage B&B.' And before she could stop herself, she'd turned into the long sweeping drive.

Milly was setting the tables for her guests' Christmas dinner when her door bell chimed.

Oh no, can't they see my no vacancy sign? It's Christmas Day! she huffed as she went to answer it.

"I'm so sorry but I don't have any spare rooms…" she started to say as she opened the door to a very pretty young woman in her twenties or thereabouts, dressed in a beautifully cut, dusky-pink coat with a faux fur collar and black patent leather boots.

"Please, I don't mind what the room is like, I just need somewhere to stay…" She burst into tears. "Oh gosh, I'm so sorry, it's just that I'm desperate…"

Milly could just hear Sophie admonishing her.

Mum, what are you doing? Don't let her in. It's Christmas Day. She's probably a con artist, after money - don't you remember that guy who befriended you and stole your painting…

Sniffling, the girl looked at her feet. Consumed with embarrassment that she'd burst into tears in front of a stranger.

But Milly sensed she was genuine… and it was Christmas Day…

"I don't have any spare rooms but if I can help you I will. What is your name?"

"Hester."

"Come in Hester. I have just made some coffee if you would like to join me?" She hadn't of course.

"Yes please," the girl stammered.

Leading her into the kitchen, she made a quick cafetiere of coffee for two, rustled up a plate of biscuits and invited her into the drawing room.

"You will find it difficult to find somewhere on Christmas Day."

"I know… it's just, I'm supposed to be staying with my boyfriend's family - I've just driven from Southampton but I'm not sure I can face it. I suffer from anxiety and they are terribly posh. No doubt I will use the wrong knife and fork at dinner or really show myself up playing some Christmas game…"

"If your boyfriend was worried about that, I'm sure he wouldn't have invited you." Milly filled her coffee cup and offered her a biscuit. "I think you will regret it if you don't go, besides they will be worried. Things are never usually as bad as one thinks."

The girl sipped her coffee silently.

"I bet your boyfriend can't wait to show you off. What is his name?"

"Julian."

"Why don't you call Julian and ask him to meet you, so you can go to the house together? It's always nice to have a little support. I don't know if you know this area, but there is a lovely little duck pond down the road where you can sit and gather your thoughts. Maybe he could meet you there and you could go for a calming walk over the fields before you meet the family. You can use my phone?"

"Oh no, it's okay, I have a mobile. I feel a lot better, please forgive me for being so stupid and barging in on you like this."

"I don't think you are stupid at all dear. Christmas can be stressful with so much pressure to be seen to enjoy ourselves and do the right thing... but I think you will feel a lot worse if you back out now..."

"You are right," the girl answered, putting down her coffee cup. "Thank you so much for your kindness."

"It is the season of goodwill." Milly attempted to joke.

"It is," she agreed.

"Promise you will call him now?"

"Promise... Merry Christmas Milly," she said making her way to the door. "Thank you again."

"Merry Christmas Hester."

I feel so much more comfortable in my own skin now that I'm old, Milly reflected as she watched her walk down the garden path and over the road towards the duck pond. *That could easily have been me, fifty odd years ago.*

Hester sat on the rickety seat opposite the duck pond. It was Christmas Day and she felt so alone.

I can't believe I did that, what's happening to me?

That lovely lady, what was she called? Milly, oh yes that was her name, she was right, I should call Julian now. Scrolling down her phone, she found his number.

"Hey babe, where are you? I thought you'd be here by now..."

"I'm just sitting by a lovely little duck pond in Fishbourne. Mills Road, I think it is, could you come and meet me?"

She wanted to tell him she was anxious, that she just needed his support to walk through that front door into his imposing family home... but he'd never understand. Julian, who was always so supremely confident in everything he did.

"Okay, I'm on my way, be with you in five..."

There was no going back now. Parking his Mercedes opposite the duck pond, Julian scooped Hester up from her seat.

"What took you so long babe?" he said, stroking her cheek.

"I got a little lost, I don't think my SatNav is the best. Would you mind if we went for a little walk across those fields? It's so pretty here," she commented, looking at the charming picture postcard thatched cottage opposite the pond. Thankfully, Julian agreed.

After a bracing walk across the fields they made their way to Julian's family home, Hester following him in her car.

"You okay babe? You are very quiet?" he asked as they walked up to the house.

"I'm fine," Hester lied, she felt so sick. Sick with nerves. *What will his parents think of me?* She fretted. His previous girlfriend was a hard act to follow, she was his sister's best friend and his mother was distraught when they split up.

"Mum, this is Hester," Julian announced as his po-faced mother opened the door.

"How do you do?" she extended her hand curtly. "We were getting worried, wondered where you were."

"Ah, she is here at last, better late than never... welcome to our humble abode," his father boomed, "What kept you? Audrey has been flapping in the kitchen..."

The dining table was awash with crystal glasses, silver tableware and stiff, starched, lace-edged, linen serviettes which scraped Hester's mouth. This was all so different to the wonderful, rambunctious Christmases she spent at home and horror of all horrors, Hester really didn't know which knife and fork to pick up first. At least Julian sensed her distress and nudged her under the table, indicating with his eyes which one she should use when. All the conversation centred around Julian and how well he was doing at work. No one even asked Hester what her job was. Then there were the family anecdotes and in-jokes. Twice, Julian's mother called her Jane, the name of his previous girlfriend which his father thought very funny. Hester tried her best, complimenting his mother on the meal and remarking how lovely the house was. They hardly acknowledged her gifts and then it was time for the dreaded Christmas games. Hester hated Charades and tried to excuse herself from any acting, preferring to guess instead. Julian's father was quite drunk and rather garrulous, insisting that she took her turn at miming. When they went on to Trivial Pursuit and Hester stumbled over an answer, he seemed to take great delight in humiliating her:

"You must know the answer to this, everyone knows it's Lake Titicaca dear. A lake in the Andes on the border between Peru and Bolivia..."

"I knew that," Julian's horrid, know-it-all, eight-year-old nephew piped up, his mother smirking. Hester's cheeks burnt with humiliation.

"Let me ask her the next question," the boy insisted, grabbing the next card, "What is the capital city of Columbia?"

Julian looked mortified at her silence. Geography was never Hester's best subject and her stumbling for an answer clearly made this child's day. The worst thing was Julian seemed utterly impervious to her distress and made no attempt to rescue her.

She couldn't wait for the night to end and when everyone went to bed, she really couldn't bring herself to say to Julian that she'd had a nice time. Not that he thought to ask. Never again would she be coerced into doing something she didn't want to do.

Especially at Christmas.

***

Richard and Zoey

Putting on her best smile, Milly stepped into the dining room to serve her guests their eagerly anticipated Christmas dinner. Candles flickered on the tables, illuminating the perfectly buffed crystal wine glasses and silver sheen of the place settings.

Richard and Zoey Peters sat at their table. A very attractive couple from London, in their early thirties. Zoey wore a lovely red velvet, knee-length dress, the perfect choice, Milly thought, for Christmas. Her auburn hair was coiled at the nape of her neck, showing off a very pretty, emerald choker and matching earrings to perfection. Her husband, Richard, who clearly adored her, was tall and dark haired with a stylish close-cropped goatee beard and moustache. Utterly charming, they greeted everyone with a cheery 'Merry Christmas,' before taking their seat in a secluded corner of the dining room.

"No regrets that we came away?" Richard squeezed Zoey's hand across the table.

"No, none." she squeezed back.
Her eye was drawn to the huge Christmas tree in the corner of the room, festooned with twinkling fairy lights and colour co-ordinated baubles. The inglenook fireplace was decorated with pine cones and clusters of seasonal holly, heavily laden with red berries.

"It's a lovely house," Zoey commented, surveying the room. "Feels like we are stepping back in time with all these beams and sloping ceilings. I can just picture some Tudor lady gathering her skirts as she climbs up that wonderful staircase in the hall."
Richard smiled, he was getting his old Zoey back. Despite, his wife's misgivings he knew it was the right thing to go away this Christmas. After their third round of failed IVF earlier in the year, they accepted the fact that they would be childless. Enough was enough. They would travel the world as a twosome; cycling over lands, sailing through

seas and zooming through the clouds. In time they would be a devoted Uncle and Auntie to all their friends and family's offspring, but not yet. They had to grieve first. Grieve for what wasn't meant to be.

Christmas with Richard's family would have been torture. After a battery of tests it was revealed that the problem lay with Zoey, and Zoey was convinced Richard's family felt she'd short-changed him. His sister, who seemed to be permanently pregnant, would be there with baby number four - a little girl called Alice, whom by all accounts was 'a happy mistake'. But Richard knew his beautiful Zoey, dying inside, would secretly smile away her pain - cuddling and cooing over the baby like everyone else. Just because it was Christmas, he wasn't prepared to put her through that.

They were so lucky to have each other, there was no other woman in the world for him. If they didn't have a family it wouldn't be the end of the world for Richard. But it was for Zoey. They would have gone abroad for Christmas but with all the travel restrictions, Richard decided he'd find them a piece of little old England where they could enjoy a quiet traditional Christmas.
On their own.

The IVF had been gruelling. Richard hated seeing Zoey inject herself every day. Then there was the mechanical, set time and date, sex. This wasn't who they were and it put a terrible strain on their otherwise very happy marriage. To rub salt in the wound, it seemed all their friends were having babies and Richard's heart ached when he watched Zoey carefully wrap yet another baby present for one of their friends. So he insisted they went away.

Zoey's eyes had lit up when Milly led them up that grand staircase to their room. Spellbound by all the nooks and crannies they passed on the way, the house was a veritable treasure trove. The dapple grey, Victorian rocking horse on the landing; wonderful old-fashioned doll's pram nestled in yet another corner and that glass cabinet full of exquisite porcelain dolls...

"That's Montmartre, isn't it?" Richard observed, looking closely at one of the pictures they passed going up the stairs.

"Yes, it is. My husband was a keen art collector, He could never go anywhere without buying a painting." Milly replied, "That was painted by one of the street artists."

"And all your rooms are named after flowers," Zoey observed.

"Yes, I don't know who named them originally but we decided to keep them. As you can see the plaques are very old."

"Here you are, you are in the 'The Wallflower," Milly said showing them in. It had a large four-poster bed, imposing walnut chest of drawers and a large Medieval style tapestry-hanging on the wall which Richard was immediately drawn to.

"If you like art, maybe you would like me to show you the brewery? A very talented young art student painted a wonderful mural down there a few years ago."

"Oh, yes please," Zoey answered, encouraging Richard to follow.

They made their way down some narrow, steep winding stairs into the adjacent part of the house, known as 'The Brewery' and there it was, covering a whole wall. Zoey gasped, it was wonderful. Three Tudor wenches were depicted serving ale inside a coaching house; a couple of horses were tethered outside, tended to by three fair-haired stable lads and a cheeky rapscallion was poking his head out of one of the upstairs windows.

"Oh wow, its beautiful," commented Zoey.

"Yes, that young girl did a very good job," Milly smiled proudly, "It could quite easily pass for a centuries old piece of handiwork."

"It certainly is very authentic looking," Richard agreed. "Quite in character with the rest of the house."

"There's a secret tunnel under here," Milly exclaimed, as she pulled up the nicely worn Turkish rug covering a rusty trap door in the floor. "It runs straight out

to the Fishbourne Marshes over the road there…
Apparently pirates used to smuggle their illicit alcohol up
here from their boats in the marshes."

"Oh my goodness," squealed Zoey in delight, "Have
you ever been down there?"

"One of the previous owners tried but they had to turn
back because the tunnel had collapsed."
It was all quite magical and Zoey would have happily
pressed Milly for more stories but time was ticking on and
they hadn't even unpacked.

***

"Penny for 'em?" Richard asked as he passed Zoey
the cranberry sauce.

"I was just wondering if there are any ghosts here, I
bet there are."

"Well, they've probably been frightened off by now,
ghosts don't like celebrations with lots of people."

"That's good, I was starting to get worried," Zoey
joked, adding in a more serious note, "Do you miss seeing
everyone this Christmas?"
Richard picked up his wife's hand and kissed her fingers,

"No," he answered resolutely, "We'll have plenty
more Christmases all together, this one is just for us… We
are picking out your special present tomorrow. Got to go
to a place called Birdham, not too far from here."

"What? Richard you've already bought me this," she
said fingering her choker lovingly.

"Yes, well, this is an extra surprise."
For the life of her Zoey couldn't think what on earth her
wonderful husband had bought her. He was so thoughtful,
always putting so much time and effort into presents for
people. If someone said they liked something he would
squirrel that information away until the time was right to
surprise them with that perfect present.

***

Madge and Oliver Wainwright

Madge and Oliver Wainwright always liked 'to make an entrance'- especially on Christmas Day. Mr Wainright sported a smart, black suit embroidered with a dazzling design of embroidered seed pearls. His wife, Madge, resplendent in a matching dress and cape, also embellished with thousands of tiny, hand-sewn seed pearls.

"Merry Christmas everyone! As a Pearly king and queen my wife Madge and I take every opportunity we can to dress up and draw attention to our charitable work. And what better day to do this than Christmas day? We look forward to seeing you all tomorrow when we depart for our special Boxing Day trip to the Witterings."
A ripple of smiles went around the room.

"Merry Christmas." Zoey and Richard raised their glass in a toast echoed by the other guests.

"You both look fantastic," Zoey added sweetly. She'd never seen such eye-catching outfits. Richard and Zoey weren't going on the Boxing Day trip and had no idea why this flamboyant couple were dressed so spectacularly. Oliver beamed at the compliment, directing his wife to her seat at their table for two.

The Wainwrights had bought an old red, London double decker bus which they used to great success - taking people out and about on fund-raising trips around London. When they mooted the idea of a special Boxing Day trip to the beach, tucking into fish and chips on board the bus, Milly instantly warmed to the idea and eagerly agreed to give her guests the option of a pre-paid trip to the Witterings - Chichester's beautiful local beach. Proceeds from the trip would go to one of Oliver and Madge's Pearly King and Queen charities. Milly's guests just had to choose which one they wanted to donate to.

The Wainwrights had a very special connection with 'Willow Cottage'. Madge had worked as a cleaning lady for Milly's young predecessor, Holly Perone. She met

Oliver, a greetings card salesman with long-standing clients in Chichester, when he stayed as a regular guest at the house and Holly never forgot how both Oliver and Madge supported her in her hour of need. The three were soon firm friends and she insisted that they had their wedding reception at 'Willow Cottage'.

Yes, here in this very dining room, reflected Madge, *Oliver and I celebrated our special day.* Madge could hear Holly now, *'Madge,* she'd insisted, *This, is your special day, relax and chat to your guests, I'm the waitress today.'*

But old habits die hard, and Madge still couldn't resist running around with the odd plate. What fun they'd had here at 'Willow Cottage', laughing at the antics of Holly's guests. Madge used to clean the rooms, puffing up the stairs with her little cleaning box. She was never very good at cleaning and Holly often had to help her put the sheets on the beds because truth be told, Madge was rather portly then. She now knew that this was down to a lot of comfort eating undoubtedly brought on by caring for her first husband, Brian. It was hard. Very hard. Nothing was ever good enough for Brian. Of course it was dreadful to see him so ill and incapacitated, so Madge turned to the comfort of regular sweet treats throughout the day. A Kit-Kat with her morning coffee and a delicious custard slice around four o'clock to keep her energy levels up. Her early evening glass of sherry - she so looked forward to a glass of Harvey's Bristol cream with a nice little shortbread biscuit or two. Extra helpings of creamy mash with her dinner and then those lovely little secret, sweet treats stashed in the fridge she'd creep downstairs for each night after Brian was tucked up in bed. And so, the pounds crept on and on and Brian was extremely unkind.

'You are a dead ringer for that Miss Piggy, Madge,' he'd say, *'You know, Miss Piggy from the Muppets… you aren't the girl I married that's for sure, that tiny waist, what was it? Twenty-two or twenty-four inches as I recall?'* And Madge would rush downstairs and raid the fridge again. Crying into her third or fourth chocolate profiterole as she tried to convince herself that he really didn't mean to be so

horrid. It was all down to that dreadful emphysema which kept him cooped up in bed. Apparently, people always took things out on their nearest and dearest…

All through their married life Madge had told him to quit smoking but he hadn't listened. A chain smoker since he was a lad of fourteen and working on the railways, he was a good forty-a-day man and these were the terrible consequences.

So Madge's little cleaning job at 'Willow Cottage' was a welcome relief from the stress and strain of caring for Brian. Of course she was distraught when he died. The early days of their marriage had been good. Brian was a good father to their daughter Phillipa and worked hard at Chichester railway station, always checking people's tickets with a smile. But he wasn't a good patient and despite her grief, Madge felt some comfort that at least she was getting a bit of her life back when he died.

Then to her astonishment, along came her beloved Oliver. He always looked so dapper, sitting at the breakfast table in his three-piece grey suit. It was funny how they got together… well, not funny for Holly.

Madge would never forget that day.

She'd let herself in with the house key which had been left in its usual place under the plant pot, with a message from Holly saying she had gone out for an early morning ride. A keen horsewoman, Holly often did this when she was stressed and Madge knew she was worried about some pretty steep upcoming expenses on the house. But when Madge let herself in she saw that Mr Wainwright's table in the dining room was still laid for breakfast, Holly clearly hadn't done any cooking that morning either. Feeling uneasy, Madge started her chores. *Why hadn't she cooked Mr Wainwrights' breakfast? There were no dirty dishes for her to collect and his two sausages which had been left out to defrost from the night before were still there, uncooked, so Holly must have been expecting him for breakfast.* Madge was starting to fret and tried to busy herself with some dusting.

An hour or so later the doorbell rang and to her horror,

Madge saw through an upstairs window that it was a policewoman. She was shaking as she ran downstairs to open the door.

"Good morning, are you Miss Holly Perone's mother?"

"No, no, I'm not, I'm her cleaning lady. Her parents live in Spain, she doesn't have any other family here. Is she alright?"

"I'm sorry to say there's been an accident and that she is in hospital. She had a nasty fall from her horse early this morning and has some concussion."

Madge had burst into tears. The police woman had to sit her down and make her a cup of tea.

"But she has guests booked in," Madge had wailed, "It's a wedding party... and what about her parents? Who is going to tell them?"

"Do you have a contact number for them?" The kindly policewoman asked.

"Their number will probably be in Holly's contact book by the telephone in the hall." Madge had sniffed. Luckily, just at that moment Mr Wainwright popped back to the house.

"Is everything alright?" he asked.

"No, Mr Wainwright, it isn't. Holly is in hospital with concussion and she has a large party of guests arriving tomorrow for a wedding party, I suppose I'd better look through her bookings book and cancel them. And what about her parents? They should be told that their daughter is in hospital..."

"Now first things first dear lady," he'd said calmly. "We will hold the fort while Holly is in hospital. She is in good hands and I am sure she will be home soon."

"Us?" Madge was speechless.

"Yes us, Madge, you can cook while I serve the breakfasts and of course I can help you with the rooms." The policewoman came back into the room with Holly's contacts book in her hand.

"I have Holly's parents' number in Spain," she'd stated, implying she would make the call.

"We can do that officer," Mr Wainright reassured her in his manly manner. "We both know Holly very well. I can assure her parents that Madge and I can hold the fort while their daughter is in hospital. No need to cancel any guests. I am in no doubt she is in good hands. We can visit her tonight and report back to her parents."

"Okay, if you are happy with that, I will put your kind offer to Holly's parents for their approval. In the meantime, I just need you to sign here," the policewoman said as she finished writing her report.

Holly's parents were more than happy they wouldn't have to dash back from Spain and pick up the reins at 'Willow Cottage'. Oliver and Madge saved the day. Love blossomed and they married a few months later.

Thinking of Holly as the daughter they never had, they were quite heart broken when she left 'Willow Cottage' for a new life in America.

Madge could still picture her lovely Holly, crouched under these same little tables scrubbing away at the glistening nocturnal snail trails before the guests came in for breakfast. Holly was so proud of 'Willow Cottage' and her thriving bed and breakfast business. Little did she know then that she too would marry one of her guests - the well-known, racing driver, Stuart Perone, who stayed at 'Willow Cottage' whenever he raced at the famous Goodwood race course.

Yes, 'Willow Cottage' had many happy memories for Oliver and Madge. Madge had always been a keen baker and while Holly was recuperating in hospital she offered a couple of Holly's guests some beautifully baked scones and cakes which proved a resounding success. This gave them the idea of starting their own little business after they got married. And so they moved to North London where they started delivering cream teas. Not long after, they were elected a Pearly King and Queen, raising money for various charities dear to their hearts and locality.

Oliver was Madge's world, and slowly and imperceptibly she became aware that she couldn't do a lot without him.

He wasn't just her husband he was her best friend. He was her everything, to the point where she couldn't face a five-minute trip to a local shop without him. Any appointments she had, Oliver had to go with her, including trips to the doctor or dentist. They joked about this to start but as time went on Oliver worried.

"Madge dear, we aren't joined at the hip, you don't need me to escort you five minutes down the road." Madge looked hurt. "But Oliver we always do everything together."

"I know dear but you don't need me to hold your hand all the time, what would happen if I wasn't here?"

"Oh don't say that Oliver, don't ever say that…" As much as he adored his wife, Oliver was starting to feel a little smothered. After discussing things with their GP, they learnt that Madge had become completely co-dependent on her husband. A condition not uncommon for people who spent a lot of time solely with each other. Madge knew he worried and knew she had to face up to the problem. But it was easier said than done. A simple errand, like going to the shop down the road was unthinkable but then when they were in the library, Madge spotted a flyer…

Just as they were finishing their Christmas pudding, Madge pushed an envelope across the table.

"Aha, what's this?" Oliver asked, picking it up. Madge reached across for his hand.

"Open it and see."
Oliver opened the envelope. It was a forty-pound receipt for a line-dancing class beginning in the New Year.

"You're not getting me dancing now are you Madge?" Oliver asked, aghast.

"No, Oliver, not you. Me. I am going on my own every Wednesday night from 7 to 9pm. It's my Christmas wish to prove to you what a strong and independent woman I'm going to be."

***

James Pemberton

James Pemberton attached his cufflinks, made sure his tie was just so and splashed a little *'Givenchy Gentleman'* on his wrists. Studying his face in the mirror above his sink he took himself to task:

I'm doing this for you and Jennifer, Evie. I would much rather have stayed at home with a good book and bung-in-the-oven Christmas dinner for one. But there you go. This is a lovely place, although I can't say I'm too enamoured about eating Christmas lunch in a room full of strangers...
One last look in the mirror, a big sigh and he made his way downstairs to the dining room.

Everybody's entrance into the dining room was staggered so Milly didn't have the stress of serving a rush of guests at the same time. A striking man in his early eighties, with a kindly smile and a full-head of beautifully cut grey hair, James Pemberton took his seat quietly at the table laid for one near the Christmas tree. His beloved wife Evelyn had passed away six months ago. No serious illness, she just didn't wake up one morning. Their daughter Jennifer and her husband, were insistent that he spent Christmas with them and their children in Cornwall but he wasn't ready for the usual, rambunctious family Christmas with unruly grandchildren greedily ripping paper off mountains of expensive presents, hardly registering what was inside they were so desperate to grab the next one. Christmas used to be magical when he was a child. He and Evelyn often used to talk about this. You never knew what you were getting. Evelyn said she could still remember Miranda, the beautiful doll in that red velvet and white fur-trimmed dress she got when she was nine. They were both appalled when Jennifer told them she was tying herself in knots trying to get everything on the children's extensive Christmas lists. Since when did children write Christmas lists? James and Evelyn had been appalled. A letter to Santa, yes, which was always sent up the chimney with a request for one very special present but a Christmas list with a whole heap of presents? Yes, Evie was his grumpy old woman and he was her grumpy old man.

Friends had been wonderful, all extending the hand of genuine friendship, wanting him to share Christmas with them but he just couldn't. How could he celebrate when his wife was hardly cold in her grave?

As he sampled the surprisingly tasty Lobster Bisque, his eye was drawn to the rather flamboyant couple sitting in the corner. He knew immediately from his days as an editor on a national newspaper, that they were a Pearly King and Queen. He'd written a story about the fascinating history of London's working class, Pearly Kings and Queens renowned for raising money for local charities. And there was no mistaking those clothes!

Madge had clearly been fretting about the lonely looking gentleman eating on his own on Christmas Day. So after Oliver had opened his surprise gift she urged her good-natured husband to extend some Christmas spirt and invite him over to their table. Ever the gentleman, Oliver was more than happy to oblige:

"Merry Christmas Sir, please, come and join us for a drink when you have finished eating." he called over.

"Well I don't want to intrude…"

"Not at all," Oliver said kindly, outstretching his hand, "Oliver Wainright, and this is my wife Madge…"

***

Rose

Giles and his mother, Rose, sat quietly in another corner of the dining room sipping their soup. His mother was always such a lady, directing the spoon in just the right direction - backwards from the centre of the bowl.

He had been nervous as he scrolled down his phone for his mother's number. It had been six months since that last dreadful conversation when he'd unceremoniously cut off their call. He knew he should have called her before but he just couldn't. Not after what she'd told him on the phone that day.

But it was coming up for Christmas, maybe it was time to bury the hatchet. He'd tapped his free hand nervously on his work desk as he rang her mobile.

"Mum, its Giles."

"Giles!" Rose wanted to cry at the sound of his voice. He cut straight to the chase:

"Look I don't want you to spend Christmas on your own, I've booked us into that B&B we used to stay in when I was little, you know, the one in Chichester?"

"Of course I remember, 'Willow Cottage'..."

"Yes, that's the one, anyway, we can go on Christmas Eve, have Christmas dinner there and go to the beach on Boxing Day. What do you say?"

Rose wanted to cry.

"I'd love that. Thank you dear. But what about your father? Won't you be seeing him?"

"No mum, I won't." Giles answered in a flat voice.

"You know you can't pick me up from here, so I could meet you at Chichester train station?"

Still all this secrecy, Giles had to work hard at suppressing the annoyance in his voice, his mother was seventy-three for gods-sake and he still wasn't allowed to know where she was living.

"Will you be okay getting a train?"

"Of course dear."

"As you wish."

"It's not me Giles, it's the rules."

"I know, I know," he snapped, "I can send you a ticket to your phone."

"That won't be necessary, but thank you dear."

"Remember it will be busy as its Christmas, you might have to book a ticket…"

Rose cried when she put down her phone. At long last she'd spoken to her boy. Something she never thought would happen again. Not after what she told him. How many times had she replayed that awful conversation over in her head.

"Mum, where the hell are you? Dad is frantic with worry".

"I'm in a women's refuge Giles."

"A women's refuge? What are you talking about?"

"Your father is violent. It's been going on for years. I've had enough and left for my own safety."

"This is stupid mother, I'm coming to get you. Where are you?"

"I can't tell you darling."

"Why not? You are my mother."

"It compromises the safety of everyone here. We can't tell anyone where we are."

"What about Dad? What will he tell everyone? This will ruin him."

"I won't be here for ever. When I have somewhere to live, I will tell you."

"Pull yourself together Mum and come home. I will talk to Dad…"

He didn't believe her and it seemed he was a lot more concerned about his father and his reputation than he was about her.

A persistent knocking at her door had interrupted her tears. Dabbing her eyes Rose had reluctantly opened it. It was Rory, the scrawny, constantly grubby little seven-year-old who lived with his mother in the next room. No doubt they'd run out of milk again.

"Why are you cryin'?" he'd asked, looking at Rose closely.

"I'm fine Rory, here, give your mum this milk." Rose gave him some in a little jug.

Five minutes later he was back.

"Yes, Rory, what's the matter?"

"Nuffink."

They both looked at each other as the child shifted awkwardly on his feet.

"Would you like to come in? I've just made some toast and tea. Ask your mum first."

"She won't care."

"Go and ask her first Rory," Rose insisted firmly as he tried to barge in.

Two minutes later he was back.

"We've got that poem fingy on our fridge," he remarked as Rose gave him some buttered toast. Written by an unknown previous inhabitant at the refuge, every woman had a copy of it in their room.

I have the right not to be battered and bruised
I have the right to feel safe in my own home
I have the right to bring my children up without fear
I have the right to voice my own thoughts and feelings
I have the right…

It still made Rose emotional when she read it.

The child was hungry and gobbled down the toast, so Rose boiled him an egg.

"Do you like reading Rory?"

"Nah, don't know how."

"Who's that?" He asked, picking up a silver framed photo of Giles.

"That's my little boy, he's grown up now. So, what are you up to today?"

"Nuffink."

There's a playground down the road. I could take you there…"

"Yeah!" he said, jumping up and down on the spot.

"Ask your mum first."

And that was the start of their friendship. That little boy

saved Rose. It was the summer holidays. Every morning
Rory would come up and have breakfast with her, then she
would take him to the playground. Rose read him stories,
took him to the library and told him stories about Giles as
a little boy. She had a purpose for facing each day.
Then one morning there was a knock at Rose's door.

"Rory's got a present for you," his mother said,
looking flushed and happy. "We're moving out today. A
two-bedroom flat with a garden."

"I'm so happy for you, that's wonderful."

"Rory, will miss you."

The child was hanging back behind his mother holding the
present, clumsily wrapped in re-used, crinkled wrapping
paper. It was a box of milk chocolates. Tears pricked at the
back of Rose's eyes and she felt a lump in her throat. Rory
flung himself in Rose's arms and started sobbing.

"I love you Rose," he wailed.

"I love you too Rory, I don't know what I will do
without you. But this is so exciting. You've got a new
house and a garden. Maybe I can come and babysit
sometimes. You know, if your mum wants to go out."

Rory's mother's eyes immediately lit up.

"Would ya?"

"Yes of course, It would be a pleasure."

Rory started jumping up and down in excitement.

"Go on mum, give Rose ya number."

Rose got her phone.

"If you could put your number in for me dear…"

"Thank you for helping us," Rory's mum whispered
as she handed Rose back her phone, "I hope you move
soon."

It was the most the girl had ever said to her and Rose was
overcome with emotion, just managing to nod her head
and smile. As she watched them walk away from the
refuge that afternoon and Rory looked up and waved to her
at her window, she forced herself not to cry. But Rory's
mother never rang and when Rose tried to call, the number
went to voice mail. So, Rose was still there in the refuge
waiting to be moved on. But for the first time in years,

Rose felt safe. Whatever she had to face here, she wouldn't jump every time she heard Basil's key in the door. She wouldn't panic in case she hadn't combed the fringes straight on the rugs in the dining room, pulled the curtains 'just so' or hung the towels in the bathroom in a specific order. She had her own little kitchenette and bathroom. She was lucky. Paint was peeling off the once white walls and there was a horrible orangey brown carpet with large swirly patterns. A small single bed in the corner of the room, a battered arm chair, a horrid cheap Formica dining table with a half-dead pot plant on it and a small TV. But it had become home.

Strangely, she didn't miss the house she first went to as a young bride. The picture postcard vicarage, with the roses around the door and rambling garden. Here, she was just Rose, the posh, old, lady who lived in Room 21. She didn't have to conceal her bruises with good old-fashioned pan stick or make excuses when someone in the village spotted she had a black eye. There were only so many times you could bump into a door. Rose was trapped in a beautiful house in a seemingly enviable life. Basil, was a vicar who with his Richard Burton type voice, delivered some wonderful sermons every Sunday to a faithful following in the village. He was a Jekyll and Hyde, charismatic yet humble in his dealings with his parishioners - forever willing to take on yet another charitable project and open up their home to regular sherry parties. A passable father to their son Giles, whom he insisted went away to boarding school from the age of seven, but behind closed doors, a vicious, controlling bully to his wife.

It was one punch too many that day and so instead of going to her usual coffee morning in the village, she'd finally faced the humiliation of revealing her bruises to PC Marion Harding at the Domestic Violence Unit in Guildford Police Station. PC Marion Harding was the first person Rose had ever opened up to.
PC Harding was horrified and immediately started ringing around for a place for Rose in a women's refuge, praying

that they would have a room free. Under Rose's watchful gaze, she rolled her eyes and sighed after every 'No'. After two hours and about twenty cups of tea later, she found her this room. A two-hour drive away. They had to grab the place and go there and then.

It was supposed to be PC Harding's afternoon off but she didn't care. She drove Rose back to the beautiful old Vicarage that had been her home for forty years and waited in the kitchen for her to grab a few essentials. There was no way she was going to put this fragile, elderly lady on a train with her small battered suitcase.

"Ready Rose?" PC Harding had asked as she parked her car in front of the shabby, Victorian house with the proliferation of buggies around the front door.

"Yes, I'm ready dear, thank you."
It pained Rose to recall how her situation upset PC Harding. The poor girl just about contained her emotions and seemed almost reluctant to let Rose out of the car.

"Remember, this is an emergency measure," she said more than once. "You'll be here a couple of months at the most…"

"I know, and thank you for everything you have done for me." Rose had answered in her perfect English diction. A tear ran down PC Harding's cheek.

"Oh God, I'm so sorry Rose. How unprofessional of me. It's just…"
Rose fished a lace-edged hanky out of her handbag.

"There you go dear, please don't cry on my account," she said gently, her wizened fingers touching PC Harding's arm.

"This shouldn't be happening to you Rose," she sniffed.

"Well, it is happening to me dear and I will just have to cope."

"I think my generation could learn a lot from yours Rose, you just get on with things, don't you? Courage in the face of adversity and all that…"

"I don't know about that dear, I should have walked away from my situation forty years ago. But what did I do? Put up and shut up. No young woman would do that now, at least, I hope not."

Truth be told, Rose had been shocked when she first walked into the refuge. The house was teeming with children. A television was blaring from one of the downstairs rooms and a grubby looking Rory came whizzing down the bannisters as they walked up the stairs.

"Rory, I told you not to do that," Gayle, the house manager, admonished him. "Where's your mum?"

"Out." He said, looking at Gayle as if she was mad.

"Who's she?" He asked, eyeing Rose, suspiciously. "She's old."

"Rory, remember your manners. This is Rose."

"Hello, young man. Yes, I am very old. You are very young. I think you are seven?"

"How'd you know?"

"You've lost your two front teeth. My little boy was seven when that happened to him. Well, I'm very pleased to meet you."

As they approached Rose's room, a young woman was yelling at her child as she frantically searched in her handbag for the key to their room.

"Shut up Nathan, you've been in my bag again, haven't you?"

A bulging nappy hung down to his ankles.

"Nathan, I told you to shut up!" She slapped his leg hard and the child yelled louder.

"Empty your bag, Chantelle," Gayle suggested, firmly but kindly.

"He's always going in my bag, I know he's had it." The girl retorted, on the verge of frustrated tears as she upturned her bag, emptying a mini rubbish heap of sweet papers, screwed up tissues and loose change on the floor.

"Sorry, Nath, Mummy's found it," she said, looking sheepish as she retrieved it from the mess.

"I'm always losing my glasses," Rose interjected sweetly, "My husband," she faltered, "My husband says I should wear them on a string around my neck."

The girl smirked as she dragged little Nathan into their room, promising him a bag of 'Wotsits.'

"Don't worry about Chantelle, she's a good girl really, just finds it hard to cope," Gayle apologised quietly as they entered the room.

Rose woke up the next morning to shouting. A child screaming and a blaring TV. *Must be Chantelle,* Rose sighed. But she'd had a good night's sleep, the best in years. As she settled into the bath, the stress melted off her shoulders as she realised how good it was to feel safe. Whatever she had to face here, it had to be better than living in fear. A thick, black cobweb was wrapped around the exposed hot water pipe leading up to the old-fashioned Ascot water heater on the wall. Basil would have gone mad at the sight of it. It was strangely comforting. A symbol of her newfound freedom.
I'm going to live with that, I'm not going to dust it away. Well, this is an adventure, she told herself as she sank into the water. But then her thoughts turned to Basil. How did he react when he read the note she left him on the kitchen table? He would never have believed she had it in her to walk away. For a moment she felt sorry for him.
How would he cook his own dinner? How would he explain her absence? He couldn't possibly tell anyone the truth. A vicar assaulting his wife?
But she only had to look at the bruises on her arm to feel angry again. It was Giles, their son, she should be worrying about, not Basil.
Giles, I'll have to tell him the truth but I can't tell even tell him where I am...

Getting out of her bath, she'd dressed and sprayed herself with the remnants of the *Blue Grass* perfume Giles gave her for her birthday. The bottle was practically empty but she wouldn't throw it away, it was too precious. Then settling herself in her room she scrolled down her phone and made that horrible call...
But now she was going to see him for Christmas. Rose's heart sang as she boarded the train to Chichester. Six

whole months since she'd seen her darling boy. Dressed in her faded blue suit, she'd taken care with her hair and make-up that morning. She so wanted to look her best and truly believed that physically she did, because since she had been away from the Vicarage, the dark shadows had gone from under her eyes and even her frown lines appeared softened.

I am so much calmer in myself, not coiled up like a tight spring ready to jump out of my skin.

As the train sped on her thoughts turned to memories of Giles' childhood. It was so thoughtful of him to choose Chichester. They often used to go there during the school holidays. A Mrs Hollis and her husband used to run it then. She always made a great fuss of Giles.

As the train drew into Chichester, Rose felt a fit of nerves. *Supposing he'd brought Basil with him? Maybe this was his way of getting them back together?*

The thought was terrifying and she pushed it to the back of her mind. Thankfully, it was just Giles, standing the other side of the ticket barrier. A little thicker around the middle maybe but he was still her boy. Enveloping her in his outstretched arms they hugged. Rose inhaled his familiar scent, wishing she could cling on to him for ever.

"Come on Mum, let me take your bags," Giles said, motioning her towards his Mazda. "Let's make our way to the B&B, we'll get checked in then maybe go out for a nice gin and tonic before dinner?"

They didn't speak much in the car, both too overcome with emotion.

'Willow Cottage' was still painted that distinctive duck egg blue Rose remembered. They'd spent so many happy little holidays here when Giles was little. Of course, Basil was always too busy to come. So it was just the two of them. Long lazy days at Witterings beach or fishing for little fish in the Fishbourne meadows just over the road from the house. Once, they had to run for their lives when they were stung by a couple of wasps. They'd settled in a secluded spot near the stream, flowing with the clearest bubbling water. It was idyllic, Giles had taken off his socks and was paddling near bunches of wild watercress growing in the water. Suddenly there was a shriek as he was stung by a wasp and made a quick dash up the bank. Rose smiled at the memory, happily, it didn't put him off going back the next day.

Giles parked the car at the end of the drive and carried their cases to the door which boasted a beautiful Christmas wreath of entwined holly, hops and pine cones. It was opened by a very pleasant lady who looked in her seventies or thereabouts.

"Hello there," she said brightly, extending her hand.

"I'm Milly, welcome to 'Willow Cottage'."

The hall was strewn with seasonal decorations and there was a lovely, welcoming, Christmassy smell of cinnamon and cloves. Clusters of holly bursting with red berries hung over the paintings going up the magnificent winding, mahogany staircase to their room. The house was pretty much as Rose remembered, albeit with a different owner. Mr and Mrs Hollis had obviously long gone to pastures new. Rose would enquire after them later.

Rose was in the 'Delphinium' room. It had a delightful little stained-glass window depicting a blue Delphinium flower. As the light shone into the room, freckles of blue light danced on the walls. Giles was next door in the yellow 'Primrose Room.'

"I can recommend both the pubs over the road if you are looking for a bite to eat, I think a few other of our guests are over there. They are a very friendly crowd." Milly smiled warmly. "Right then, I will leave you to get settled. I look forward to seeing you both in the dining room around twelve tomorrow, for some smoked salmon blinis and a glass of champagne. Have a lovely evening."

"Sounds wonderful." Rose smiled.

"It certainly does," Giles agreed.

Rose couldn't remember the last time she'd been out and she was so proud to be on the arm of her son. She'd dismissed this Christmas, anticipating that she would be on her own in the refuge.

Being here with her son was more than she ever dared wish for. Walking down the path from 'Willow Cottage' they crossed the road and went into the 'Bull Head' - a charming olde-worlde pub with a classic, Sussex-style thatched roof. Teeming with a jolly, crowd of locals, a huge log fire cackled invitingly as everyone got into the Christmas spirit. Pictures of country scenes adorned the walls with sprigs of holly and trailing silver streamers. Giles directed Rose to a more private, cosy corner of the pub, close to the fire, while he went to the bar to order their drinks.

"There you go Mum," he said putting two gin and tonics on the table. "So, how have you been?"

Rose could feel his eyes studying her intently.

"Fine dear, fine."

"I know you can't tell me where you are but is the place okay?"

"Yes, dear. I have my own kitchen and bathroom, unlike a lot of the other women who have to share. The perk of being old," she tried to joke.

"I hate the thought of you being there, how has this happened Mum?"

Rose took a deep breath.

"I wish I knew dear, I've often thought it was my fault and that I'd brought things on myself but I now know that is wrong. A man should never strike a woman whatever the provocation." She added sternly.

"I still can't believe it Mum. Of course Dad has denied everything but I spoke to Audrey and she told me she'd known for years."

"Audrey?" Rose asked aghast, their neighbour for the last thirty odd years. Rose had never uttered a word to her.

"She told me she knew something was wrong, people had noticed the bruises Mum."

A sick feeling of bile crept up Rose's throat.

How humiliating.

"She is very concerned about you Mum and feels terrible that you felt you couldn't confide in anyone."

Rose's natural instinct was to block the rest of this conversation and just go through the motions of listening to what her son was saying.

"These situations are always very difficult," Rose said simply, swirling the remnants of the ice cubes in her drink.

"So when did this start?"

"Not long after we married. I don't remember exactly when."

She did of course. Basil had pushed her down the stairs after an argument about the way the towels were displayed in the bathroom. Rose was pregnant with their first child and miscarried. She nearly left him then but had nowhere to go. Her resentment and fragile state following the miscarriage added fuel to the fire. She was terrified all the time she was pregnant with Giles - constantly fearful the same thing would happen. Causing her to retreat even further from her husband.

"Mum?"

"Sorry dear, we will talk about this but it's Christmas Eve and I am so pleased to see you, let's not spoil things. Please tell me all about what you have been up to?"

Giles knew that for the moment he was beaten, so with a heavy sigh, he told her all about his not very exciting life, which mainly consisted of going to work in a job he tolerated, but despite Rose's reluctance to open up to him, it had been a good evening. They tucked into some excellent, locally sourced sausages with Giles insisting that they topped the evening off with the butterscotch pudding. Rose had a definite spring in her step as they walked arm in arm in companionable silence back up the path to 'Willow Cottage'. This was going to be a wonderful Christmas; Giles was the best present she could ever wish for.

***

Stephen

Milly peeked at her guests through the crack in the kitchen door. Everything seemed to be progressing nicely.

Mr Pemberton was having a drink with Madge and Oliver at their table. Nazim and Moola were showing Maryam how to pull a Christmas cracker, while little Karim was gurgling happily in his highchair.

Richard and Zoey were holding hands across the table, Rose and Giles laughing at each other in their paper hats. Each table boasted a lovely Christmassy table decoration with a seasonal candle in the centre. Larger ivory, church style candles were flickering nicely in the inglenook fireplace with Milly's six-foot Christmas tree sparkling in the corner of the dining room.

***

Milly worried for the young man in the 'Gardenia' Room who insisted he didn't want to come down for Christmas dinner.

Stephen Montague was aged around thirty, smartly dressed and the owner of a very desirable E-type Jaguar.

"If it's okay with you Mrs Henderson, I'd prefer to stay in my room, I have some choice Christmassy bits from Waitrose," he said, indicating the bulging carrier bags sitting on the window sill. "All I want to do is relax and enjoy some Christmas TV in this lovely room."

"I could bring you up your dinner on a hot plate, it's no trouble."

"That's very kind but I will be fine, thank you so much anyway."

"Is there anything else I can get you?"

"An ice bucket would be nice, I have rather a nice bottle of Sancerre… and maybe a wine glass?" he grinned, showing off perfectly spaced, white teeth.

"Of course, coming up."

"Oh no, please, Mrs Henderson, I don't want you running up and down the stairs after me, I can come down and get them later." He clearly didn't want to chat, politely thanked Milly again and retreated into his room.

What a delightful young man he is, I do wish Sophie was here. She'd be sure to get him downstairs... Milly fretted.

But he seemed happy enough with all his Christmas snacks and TV at the ready, it just seemed wrong somehow, him shut up in his room on his own. He didn't even come down for Milly's special champagne brunch and bypassed the Christmas Eve drinks party in the dining room. He appeared to be such an easy-going, sociable young man too but, one had to respect people's feelings.

Milly could just hear Bill admonishing her:

Leave him alone darling, he's clearly wants to be on his own. People can have a good Christmas with just them-selves for company you know? I know I did in the past.

Then Milly started to fret that this Stephen Montague was a young widower, just like Bill had been.

Oh no, all I've done is barge in on his grief... it didn't bear thinking about.

Happily, Stephen Montague wasn't a young widower. But unhappily, as tempting as a champagne brunch that morning sounded, he could hardly face himself, let alone the other guests. Celebrating Christmas was the last thing on earth he wanted to do. His life had gone into free fall this last year. He'd lost his job, his girlfriend and his flat. He was addicted to gambling - horse racing mostly but also on-line poker and the odd scratch card. Soon he'd have to crawl back home to his parents because he was effectively homeless. How had this all happened? What had gone so terribly wrong? Pulling the ring on a mini-can of gin and tonic which he'd chilled in the sink, he lay back on one of the comfy duck-down pillows as it all came flooding back in vivid technicolour.

'Steve, you just aren't cutting the mustard mate.' Ben, his work colleague and fellow trainee at the law firm where he worked lectured him in no uncertain terms. *'You gotta be seen to put the hours in. I did eighty hours last week. That's why I camp in the office...'*

Two months later Ben had hurled himself to his death from the roof top of a well-known London restaurant. After a working lunch with a couple of colleagues, like so many he'd had before, no one suspected anything was wrong. He just got up from the table, walked out to the roof garden and did it.

So many nights Stephen had tossed and turned going over conversations they had in his head, looking for clues. Ben had always seemed so in control, he was the last person Stephen thought would do such a terrible thing. *'Look mate,'* he'd said, swirling the ice in his gin glass, just a week or so before he killed himself, *'It won't be like this for ever. We've just gotta bite the bullet, put the hours in and then we'll be set for life - eh partner?'* he'd joked. Stephen had tried, managing sixty-one hours one week.

His girlfriend, Ginny, a trainee banker was just as driven in her work. Sometimes it felt as though it was a competition - who could clock up the most hours at work? But Ginny was a high flier, she liked the nice things in life. Like him, she came from an impoverished family the wrong side of town. Money and status was everything to Ginny. Expensive holidays, weekends away. Designer clothes. These were the things that defined you, she said, and they didn't come cheap.

'You are burning yourself out Ginny'… he'd dared to comment as she was throwing a black coffee down her throat before dashing out the door at six am that morning. *'Get a grip Steve,'* she snapped, *'We're young, we can handle it. There's a lot of competition out there and I for one, don't want to miss out when it comes to promotion,'* she added nastily.

After Ben's death Stephen didn't think twice about jacking everything in. The sight of Ben's empty desk was unbearable and another willing recruit soon took up his space. His so-called ambition had killed his friend. Of course, Stephen couldn't tell Ginny that he'd quit his job, she assumed he was still going to work every morning.

My God, he mused, *I can't believe I kept up the façade of going to work every day - and for six months too.*
Instead of getting the tube every morning, he'd make a bee-line for the little café around the corner; have a flat-white coffee, study the day's racing and place his bets. But of course it all came out in the end. Ginny bumped into one of his colleagues and he was rumbled. Things went from bad to worse between them and she threatened to tell his parents, that horror of all horrors, their golden boy was unemployed. That was unthinkable, the first one to go to university in his family, his mum and dad had been so proud - *'Our Steve, a lawyer in a posh London firm.'* It would break their hearts. He couldn't come clean.

It wasn't long before he couldn't pay his half of the mortgage and Ginny gave him an ultimatum.
'Sort yourself out by Christmas or we're finished.'

'Why aren't you coming for Christmas son?' His mother had wailed on the phone.
'Ginny booked us a surprise trip to the Caribbean Mum,' he lied.
'But Steve, all the children will he here...'
This was another problem. Uncle Steve always splashed the gifts - expensive spa days and perfume for his mother and sisters, the latest computer games or must-have toy for his nieces and nephews, something expensive and usually useless for his Dad. Uncle Steve was a hotshot London lawyer and Christmas wasn't Christmas without 'Santa Steve' showering everyone with gifts. He just couldn't face them without the eagerly anticipated Santa sack. And so with a heavy heart, he booked himself into Willow Cottage. No one would know him here. It felt good to be anonymous.

***

It was a good time for Milly to give her guests their token gift from the tree. One of the local book shops came up with the entertaining idea of selling books neatly wrapped in brown paper and string, with the inscription '*Your Date with a Book*'. The customer had no idea which book they were buying until they opened it. At just a few pounds each it was a fun idea that went down a treat with Milly. It would be a talking point for her guests, bringing them together at a time of celebration. So she bought one for all of them - adding a hand-written tag with their name and the inscription '*Merry Christmas from Willow Cottage.*' Stepping into the dining room Milly took a deep breath.

"Merry Christmas everyone, if you have finished your meal, I would like to invite you to the Christmas tree where you'll see I have placed a book amongst the branches with your name on it. I have no idea what it is, it is just a bit of Christmas fun. You may love it, you may loathe it, either way please feel free to swap with another guest."

"What a lovely idea," Madge smiled.

"Now maybe we should start with our youngest guests first. Maryam darling, if you and Karim would like to come to the tree…"

Nazim translated, encouraging his daughter to take her little brother's hand and walk over to Milly.

"There you go," Milly said, taking down a brightly wrapped package with a silver bow from the tree for Maryam, who clutched it protectively to her chest.

"This was one of my favourite books when I was little girl. "Now, what can we find for Karim?"

Milly went through the motions of poking amongst the branches and retrieved another brightly wrapped package. Placing it in Karim's chubby little hands, she bent down and whispered in his ear, "Happy Christmas Karim."

All eyes were on the children as they opened their gifts at their table with Nazim and Moola.

"Bless them," Madge commentated to Oliver, tears in her eyes.

"Yes, bless the little darlings," Oliver, had trouble containing the emotion in his voice.

Zoey nestled closer to Richard:

"How lovely, they will never forget their first Christmas will they?"

"No, I don't think they will," Richard agreed, his voice breaking.

Moola held up the books for everyone to see.

"Thank you, Father Christmas, so much. Maryam has *Peter Rabbit* by Beatrix Potter and Karim, *Guess how much I love you*? These books will always be very special to them."

Mr Pemberton burst into spontaneous applause and was soon joined by everyone else. There was hardly a dry eye in the room. This was indeed, a very special Christmas.

Not wishing to make a song and dance of inviting Moola and Nazim to the tree when they were showing the children their books, Milly quietly passed them their gift from the tree. A jar of specially wrapped, *Fortnum & Mason* breakfast marmalade.

"You spoil us Milly, thank you from the bottom of our hearts," Nazim hugged her. "How did you know how much we love your English marmalade?"

"Well, Moola told me how much you all enjoy your croissants in the morning so I thought some English marmalade to go with them would be a safe bet." Milly smiled, a twinkle in her eye.

"Thank you, dear Milly," Moola reiterated, on the verge of tears.

Madge sensed Milly wanted to sit with the family and spend a little time showing the children the pictures in their books.

"Would you like me to take over at the tree for a bit?" she called over, "I can see you can't resist reading a story..."

"If you wouldn't mind Madge?"

"Of course not, just call me Mother Christmas," she joked. "Now, this one is for you, Mr Pemberton."

"Thank you so much, I'm looking forward to seeing what it is," he said, making a bit of a performance opening the tightly wrapped brown paper package...

"Ahha, it's *The Spy who Loved Me* by Ian Fleming. Capital, I always saw myself as Q," he laughed, "Thank you Santa."

"And here's yours Oliver," Madge beamed, handing him his present.

"What do you have there?" Zoey enquired.

"Sherlock Holmes, By Arthur Conan Doyle, wonderful, we really enjoyed the film didn't we Madge?"

"We did... and I love Robert Downey Jnr," Madge cooed.

"Me too," Zoey agreed.

"Ooh mine's *'Two of a Kind'* by Clare Cassy. A steamy, Spanish romance by the look of it." Zoey read out loud from the blurb at the back, *When Juanita Estevez crosses paths with Santi Alvarez, their worlds are turned upside down as they realise they are two of a kind... can they ever get together and if so, how?* I like the sound of this!"

"And mine's *'Love your Garden'* by Alan Titchmarsh Madge responded, 'Sounds a bit more you than me dear, fancy doing a swap?"

"What's mine is yours." Oliver teased.

"What did you get?" Zoey smiled at Rose as she unwrapped her book.

"*Some of me poems*, by Pam Ayers, I used to love her TV show, thank you so much Santa," she smiled at Milly.

"Go on, your turn," Rose prompted Giles, "Don't keep us waiting."
Giles unwrapped his gift. "*English Vineyards* by Veronica Burton "Great, I visited a wonderful one in Sussex last year, I will look forward to reading this," he said looking at the cover.

"And last but not least, Richard." Milly handed him his package. Zoey, smiled with her eyes as she watched her beloved husband go through the motions of unwrapping his gift.

"*DIY on a budget*, well that's perfect for me," he smiled, raising his glass in thanks to Milly.

And so the good-natured banter continued, with everyone getting into the Christmas spirit.

"And where's yours Milly?" Madge asked, "Santa included you I hope."

"He did," Milly laughed as everyone watched her tackle the wrapping paper.

"I got '*Fifty Shades of Grey*'!!"

***

Gwen

There was another guest squirreled away at the top of the house, who told Milly in no uncertain terms, that she too, wouldn't be coming down to Christmas dinner.
Gwen Cartwright was a writer around the same age as Milly who had become, over the years, as much a friend as a paying guest. 'Willow Cottage' was something of a retreat for her when she was in need of inspiration or emotional escape. She always insisted on staying in the 'Heliotrope Room,' right at the top of the house. It had a wonderful view over the garden and she used to write with her laptop perched on her knees, sitting on the window seat.

"It has to be the 'Heliotrope Room' Milly, because as you know, that's where I wrote '*The Honey Trap*' - my most successful book."

A single lady, she had no immediate family although she did have a rather elusive partner called Simon, whom she had known for twenty-odd years.

"He did invite me to spend Christmas with him and his daughters Milly," Gwen fibbed, "But I just couldn't stand the thought. They are intolerable - quite ghastly. I really can't bear to be around them. I think they think I am after their father's house - bloody cheek, it's not my taste at all - a horrid little box, a real throwback to the sixties…"
But the sad truth was that Simon was a married man, and Gwen was always alone at Christmas, not to mention countless other special occasions. Despite his promises over the years, divorce was never on the cards and he was always very reluctant to meet her friends. Gwen would always be his mistress. Her friends had given up asking about him and no one could understand why she would choose to waste her life on someone who made her so miserable.

"Well, are you sure you are alright up here on your own? I can bring you up something," Milly offered.

"No dear, I am fine, I have my characters for company, they keep me very busy as I never know until I bang on the keys quite what they are getting up to next. I will join you on the trip to the beach tomorrow though."

"Well, if you are sure." Milly was far from convinced that Gwen was alright and she certainly hadn't fallen for the story about her being invited to spend Christmas with the daughters, as a mutual friend let on that Simon's wife was still very much in evidence.

She's covering up like she does every Christmas. She looks so tired and drawn. If only she would see sense.

My characters do keep me company, Gwen mused sadly, as Milly shut her door and went downstairs. *But not on Christmas Day. Today I need to be with someone who wants to be with me and that isn't Simon.* As she gazed forlornly out the window her phone pinged with a text message.

Happy Christmas my darling Gwen, My heart aches for you. What do you say to a week in Florence or Rome? My New Year Treat…

How convenient mobile phones were when one was a cheat. It was so easy to text. Gwen could just visualise him doing it at the dining table while his wife was preparing their feast in the kitchen... and she was furious. How dare he treat her *and* his wife in such a way? Each year he did the same. Gwen had spent countless miserable Christmases on her own. Then he'd sweep her off her feet with a couple of weeks somewhere sunny. And she always fell for his lies.

Well, not this year. After twenty years together, she'd finally seen the light. And it hurt.

***

Moola and Nazim, Maryam and little Karim

The last guests to come into the dining room were Moola, Nazim and the children. Nazim had been an interpreter for the British army in Kabul while his wife Moola had run her own beauty salon. They'd arrived in England with little more than the clothes they were wearing and had been staying with Milly for around eight weeks. They had been lucky. They'd survived the terrifying crush at Kabul airport, passing their children up over their heads into the arms of the British soldiers frantically trying to contain the surging crowds of desperate people as their papers were checked at the barrier.

They'd been lucky. So lucky. They'd escaped the Taliban.

All eyes were on the family as they came into the dining room. Nazim bowed graciously to everyone in the room, wishing them a very Happy Christmas. Maryam was dressed in traditional dress like her mother, the younger child, aged about eighteen months old and his father were dressed in more Western style clothes.

James Pemberton was mesmerised by the family, he was pretty sure that that they were from Afghanistan. The children were so quiet and well behaved, the parents so gracious. And after everything they had been through. Images of those awful scenes of people rushing on to the runway at Kabul airport, clinging on to the wheels of aircraft in a desperate attempt to escape the invading Taliban, flashed through his mind.

He noticed that the little girl was gazing at the Christmas tree throughout their meal and after they finished their Christmas pudding, Milly wandered over and asked the mother if she could take her daughter over to the tree. Milly encouraged the little girl to take down a chocolate for her and her little brother before she shyly returned to the table with her family. The father then brought the baby over to the tree and showed him the sparkly hanging ornaments. His little chubby hand reaching out to touch a hanging snowman.

Milly had left a couple of board games out in the communal sitting room in case any of her guests wanted to play a game or watch some Christmas television. The dining room was emptying and she started collecting the dishes. Moola collected up her family's plates, intent on making her way to the kitchen to help Milly.

"Don't worry Moola, you are busy with the children. I can do this."

"No, Mrs Milly, let me help you," she insisted, a pile of plates in her hand.

"My wife insists," Nazim echoed, "I can look after the children, let Moola help you Mrs Milly, it's the least we can do after such a wonderful English Christmas dinner." And with that he made his way into the sitting room with the children.

"You are very naughty," Milly joked as she stacked the dishwasher and Moola brought out more plates. "How are you settling into your new life?"

"Very well Mrs Milly, we are so thankful to be here in your wonderful country and this beautiful house, so very lucky." Her lip quivered and she burst into tears.

"Oh Moola, put those dishes down, come, let's sit down."
Ushering Moola back into the dining room, Milly closed the door and they sat down at one of the tables.

"I am sorry Mrs Milly," she sobbed.

"You have nothing to apologise for. You have been through so much." Milly put a protective hand over hers.

"It's just that I miss my family and am so worried about them. Sometimes I feel guilty that we got out and they didn't. My parents, four sisters and two brothers are still there. I don't know what's become of them, if they are all safe from the Taliban. One of my sisters is a teacher, and she isn't allowed to work, the Taliban only allow male teachers to teach in schools now. Her daughters cannot go to school. My older sister is a judge. She sent many evil people to prison, who have now been released by the Taliban. She has received death threats from them and has had to leave her house."

"Oh Moola, I am so, so sorry."

"Another one of my brothers was also an interpreter for the British and Americans. I don't know why but he hasn't got out despite all the promises made to him…" she sniffed, "And I had to leave my beauty salon. The Taliban defaced my shop window, they disapprove of women wearing make-up and uncovering their hair. I had three women working for me and I just had to shut up shop and leave. We all had to go into hiding. I don't know what has happened to them Mrs Milly."

Milly didn't know what to say, all she could do was sit with this devastated young woman in companiable silence. Words seemed so trivial.

"You know, like me, a lot of my friends could do with updating their look Moola. We've all worn the same lipstick and eye shadow for the last twenty years," she squeezed her hand. "You made such a good job of my make-up, introducing me to blusher and primer under my foundation…" she smiled, "So why don't I get a few of them round one afternoon? We will all pay the going rate."

"Oh no, Mrs Milly, you don't have to pay me, it would be my privilege…"

"Yes, Moola, we do need to pay you." Milly said firmly. "This is your work. Word gets around and I think you could do very well here in Chichester, so that's something to think about isn't it?" she gave her hand a squeeze.

Moolas eyes lit up, "I would like very much to do your make up again Mrs Milly, you are very beautiful and I am sure your friends are too."

"Good," Milly smiled, "I will get a few of them round. Now you go and join your husband and beautiful children while I finish in the kitchen."

And despite her protests Milly managed to chivvy her into the living room.

Little Karim was fast asleep on the sofa sandwiched between Oliver and Madge, while Maryam and her father were setting up a game of Snakes and Ladders with Mr Pemberton.

"I used to play this game every Christmas when my daughter Jennifer was a little girl. Now take a coloured counter and put it here." Mr Pemberton was in his element. Maryam and her father did as directed. Both listening intently to his instructions as Moola came into the room.

"May I introduce you to my wife James?" Nazim said proudly, standing up from his chair. "Moola, this is James."

"I am delighted to meet you," James answered. "Would you like to join us for a game of Snakes and Ladders? Your daughter is learning fast, so be warned," he teased.

Moola looked across at little Karim.

"I would like that yes, but…"

"It's okay dear," Madge spoke up, "Your little one is fine here with us. There's nothing like playing a good Christmas game, you carry on."

"Well, if that is alright with you?"

"Of course it is dear."

Maryam's eyes lit up when she saw that her mother was going to join them and excitedly passed her a yellow counter.

"Here Mama, take this counter and put it here. You are yellow, I am blue, Baba is green and Mr Pemberton is red," she beamed proudly.

James explained the rules. First to throw the dice was Maryam.

"Now, you throw the dice and move your counter like this… You got a five so you move your counter along five places. Ahha, you have landed on a ladder, so you go up to number 14. Well done Maryam!"

Maryam was overjoyed and clapped her hands. "Your turn now Mr Pemberton!"

"So it is, remember, if you throw a six you get an extra turn!" James Pemberton shook the dice and moved his counter the required number of places.

"Oh dear, I've landed on a snake," he said theatrically. "Down I go…"

Moola felt a warm glow. She hadn't heard her little girl laugh in so long.

James Pemberton was happy too. Maybe this wasn't such a bad Christmas after all. Little Karim had woken up and was bouncing happily on Madge's knee, laughing as Oliver made peek-a-boo faces at him. Rose and Giles were reading their books from the Christmas tree.

As Milly offered everyone more mince pies, she too felt happy. Happy that she'd created a little Christmas cheer for these people who, with the exception of Oliver and Madge, she sensed were a little lost and lonely like her.

Mr Pemberton, Moola and Nazim were chatting amiably. Oliver and Madge were clearly delighted to have children about. Rose and Giles were spending quality time with each other. Even Gwen and that strange young man upstairs appeared to be enjoying Christmas within the walls of her home. Despite all her family protests, it was the right thing to open up 'Willow Cottage' this Christmas.

"Would you like to try a mince pie dear?" Milly asked little Maryam. The little girl was standing in front of Milly's dolls house in the corner of the room. She shook her head shyly.

"Would you like to see inside my doll's house?" The child nodded.

Milly carefully unlatched the front panel of the green, three story, Victorian house to reveal the rooms inside. Her pride and joy, it wasn't really a toy and Milly had always forbidden her grandchildren to play with it, but she could sense that this little girl would treat it with the respect it deserved. Maryam gasped, her eyes as large as saucers as Milly showed her each exquisitely furnished room.

"This is the dining room," Milly said, "And here is the butler who serves the food to the family."

A real, gold rimmed, miniscule, blue porcelain china dinner service was laid out on the carved, mahogany dining table, complete with silver candle sticks and silver serving platters.

"This is the nursery where the dolls play." Milly pointed out the dapple-grey rocking horse with his white tail and mane. "This is the Mother and Father's bedroom." An ornate, four poster bed was made up with satin sheets and pillows with a multi-coloured crocheted coverlet. There was an exquisite little dressing table and gilt mirror with a tiny velvet, heart-shaped jewellery box. A real emerald chip necklace inside it. As the little girl's eyes wandered through the house, Milly encouraged her to pick up one of the dolls. Maryam chose the little girl wearing the frilly Victorian dress and blue sash.

"Would you like to play with her Maryam?"
The little girl nodded so Milly left her alone and joined Oliver and Madge on the sofa with little Karim who had fallen asleep again, this time in Madge's lap.

"He's gorgeous isn't he?" Madge whispered, stroking his black curls.

"He is," Milly agreed, "Hopefully he won't remember much about how he came to live in the UK."

"Let's hope not," Madge agreed. "It makes you realise how lucky we all are."

"It does indeed," Milly acquiesced, noticing that Oliver was napping next to them.

"Oh, I wish he were our grandson," Madge commentated, "I just love babies this age. But I don't think my Phillipa will oblige," she added stoically.

"You may be surprised," Milly added, "I never thought Sophie would have a child, she was so busy going on tour all the time waiting for that big break in the music world... but then she had Hope, no one was more surprised than me."
As Milly and Madge continued their conversation, Moola crossed the room to join her daughter at the doll's house.

"Can I play with you my darling?" she whispered.

"It's okay, Mama, I'm fine on my own."
Moola was happy to see her daughter could still play like the little girl she really was. She had seen so much in her nine years on this earth. Things that no child or adult should ever witness.

Maryam was in her own little world, totally absorbed in playing with the doll's house.

I wish this was our house, she said to herself, as she moved the dolls from room to room. She put the old lady doll in the rocking chair by the fire in the playroom. *She is like my Manani,* she thought sadly, rocking the miniature chair back and forth with her finger. There were so many teeny toys in the room; dolls with their own dolls, a train, minute books with pictures and words. The letters were so different to the script Maryam used in school. Picking up the little doll she put her on the rocking horse, then made her push the doll's pram around the room.

I had one like this is Afghanistan, and books I could read and a grandmother and a grandfather and cousins and aunties and uncles...

From the playroom, she made her way to the kitchen where tiny shiny pots and pans hung from the ceiling. A mini trestle table was adorned with an assortment of silver platters and tiny dishes laden with chicken, pies and vegetables in the centre of the table. There was a porcelain sink with a scrubbing brush, an Aga cooker with pots and a kettle on it and a dog nearby curled up in a basket. Tears filled her eyes as she thought of their dog, Babic. He had to be left behind too. Climbing the mother doll up the stairs to her bedroom, she picked up the heart-shaped jewellery box with the emerald necklace displayed inside. *Mama had lots of jewels like this is Afghanistan, she used to show them to me and I would try them all on - bangles and bracelets, earrings and rings...*

"Maryam, it's time to go to bed now," Moola interrupted her play. "This is a very beautiful dolls house," she commented, peering inside one of the rooms.

"Mama, look, this is a real necklace just like the ones you had at home."

"Yes it is," Moola answered sadly, because apart from a couple of rings and a necklace, most of it had been left in Afghanistan. "Come on now, say good night to everyone Maryam and thank you to Mrs Milly for letting you play with her beautiful house."

Moola stooped to pick up Karim from Madge's lap.

"Thank you so much for looking after him."

"It's a pleasure it really is," Madge cooed stroking Karim's curls.

"A fine little fellow you have there," Oliver added, waking up from his snooze.

"Thank you for letting me play with your dolls house." Maryam hugged Milly.

"My pleasure Maryam, all the dolls were waiting for a little girl like you to play with them. Would you like to play with it again?"

Maryam nodded her head.

***

The Beach

"All aboard," Madge joked as she stood in her bus conductor outfit welcoming everyone on the bus on Boxing Day morning.

"Here's your ticket young lady," she beamed, whizzing round the handle on the old-fashioned ticket machine she wore around her neck. And there's one for you, and one for you, and you," she said, ripping each ticket off at their perforated edges with a proud flourish. Oliver was in the driver's seat, decked out in his bus driver's uniform. The engine revved and they were off, the huge wheels of the bus slowly crunching down 'Willow Cottage's drive-way.

It was a nice crisp day. Perfect for a bracing walk on the beach. Milly was sitting next to Gwen at the front of the bus.

"Well, I don't think I've ever done this on Boxing day."

"No, me neither," Gwen giggled. "It's certainly different... sweet couple your Oliver and Madge."

"Yes, they are," Milly agreed. "They met when Madge worked here for the previous owner."

"No?" Gwen's eyes lit up, sensing a story... "Do tell, Milly dear..."

James Pemberton was sitting next to Nazim. What a fine young man he was, so proud of his little family and so willing to turn his hand to anything to give them a comfortable, secure life here in the UK. They had talked a lot last night. James would put his thinking cap on, there must be something he could do to help him find some work that was worthy of his talents. Just as James was shifting through his mental list of any possible contacts he could put Nazim's way, his phone pinged with a message from his daughter.

Happy Boxing day, Dad. You okay? What are you up to?
Happy Boxing day, darling... I'm sitting on a bus going to the beach.

The beach?

Yes, it's all rather fun… the lady who runs the B&B organised a little Boxing Day trip. We are all sitting in an old double decker London bus. Once we are parked up we are going for a bracing walk followed by fish and chips on board the bus. Your old dad is being sociable.

That's great. I'm so proud of you Dad…

No one was more surprised than James that he had allowed himself to enjoy himself. It felt good.

"Does this bring back memories?" Rose asked Giles, as she snuggled further into the collar of her coat at the front of the bus.

"It does, I used to love going to the beach."

"Special days weren't they?"

"They were, Mum."

"Thank you for a lovely Christmas darling, it was so thoughtful of you to bring me here."

"My pleasure Mum, I'm really happy you came."

"Me too." Rose squeezed his hand. She wondered if she should ask about Basil but decided against it. Why spoil things?

"Right now everyone," Madge announced standing up from her seat as Oliver parked the bus in a layby facing the beach. "Our little café is upstairs. Everyone up for fish and chips?"

A happy collective mumble clearly signified everyone was.

"Good, Oliver and I will get the fryer on, so if you could all get back here in forty minutes or so we should have everything ready."

"Can I help you?" Milly hung back, the last to get off the bus.

"Definitely not Milly, you have done enough cooking this Christmas, now go and get some sea air into your lungs," Madge said, playfully shooing her off the bus.

The air felt so sweet and fresh. Moola tucked her arm into Nazim's as they made their way down to the sea. Maryam was running wildly ahead, while little Karim was perched on Nazim's shoulders. The further Maryam ran away from them, the more nervous Moola felt. She wasn't used to her child running free.

"Maryam, Maryam wait for us," she called frantically.

"It's ok Moola, let her run, we can see her," Nazim assured her.

Moola knew he was right but it was hard to let her daughter go. With the daily scenes of carnage outside their house, then the torturous journey to the airport, Moola had kept her daughter close. Since the Taliban took over, people stayed at home. Gone were the days of going out to the playground or playing outside with friends. It was just too dangerous. There was a lump in her throat as she watched her little girl just being a little girl, throwing pebbles in the sea and jumping back from the ripples of incoming waves. She had lost so much of her childhood.

Giles and Rose, ambled along, stopping to sit on a bench and people-watch for a bit. A lot of people were out, in all probability walking off their Christmas dinner. Giles braced himself:

"Mum, we need to talk about where you are going to live."

"Can we discuss this after our little holiday darling?" Rose reiterated. "We're having such a lovely time let's not spoil things."

"Mum, if you can't have this conversation for your-self, then have it for me... you can't be happy living in secrecy with a bunch of strangers." He had to work hard at keeping the anger out of his voice. "Surely you want more for yourself?"

Rose fixed her faded blue eyes on her beloved boy and her heart ached for him and his pain at her unenviable situation.

"I understand your frustration Giles, I know you care about me and this must be very difficult for you. It may not be the greatest place after the comfort of the Vicarage but, believe me, I am a lot happier in the refuge. Things take time. As you know we don't own the house, it belongs to the church. Once your father retires it will go to his successor. There's no money there."

Giles choked back tears.

"Then come and live with me."

"No darling, you are a young man, you don't want your old mother living with you."

"Yes, I do actually," he didn't sound totally convinced.

"No darling," she put her hand on his. "I can tell you what I have done. I am eligible for social housing and given my age I can request to live near a relative. And of course, I have asked to live near you."
Giles looked genuinely relieved.

"That's good Mum, very good. I'm still going to arrange for you to see a solicitor, you need to know your rights. Dad owes you and things need to be sorted out."

Unbeknown to Giles, Rose had already seen a solicitor who told her there was no magic wand he could wave for her. The best advice he could give was that she should approach the Church and ask, given her circumstances, what help they could give her financially. *'After all, Charity begins at home,'* he attempted to make light of the situation. This was something Rose would never do. She had her pride, she wasn't going to present herself as a charity case. She wasn't even bothered about getting any money from Basil. She had no idea if he had any secret funds squirrelled away and really didn't care. He had always pleaded poverty throughout their marriage. Rose never had a housekeeping allowance like her friends. Basil made her write a list of things they needed each week and go cap-in-hand to him if she wanted anything extra for Giles. *Let him keep his stinking money. I have my health, my sanity and our son. These are the important things.*

Milly checked her watch.

"We'd better make our way back," she said to Gwen as they crunched along the pebbly part of the beach.

"Hungry?"

"Yes, I am a bit."

"How's the writing going?"

"Slowly," Gwen remarked dejectedly. "I wanted to write something new, you know, deviate from my usual subject matter but I don't know Milly, the creative juices seem to be drying up… who is that young man over there looking so pensively out to sea? He was sitting at the back of the bus wasn't he?"

"He's from London, wanted to spend Christmas on his own, like someone else I know…"
Gwen smiled.

"Well as one loner to another, I'm going to go over and introduce myself. See you back at the bus!"

"Welcome to our café," Madge beamed as everyone climbed the stairs to the top deck. All the old bus seats had been taken out and it had been cleverly transformed by Oliver into the most delightful café sporting half a dozen tables and chairs cleverly fixed to the sides and floor of the bus. He'd even installed a neat looking galley kitchen and was frying fish in a deep fat fryer, thick golden chips sizzling happily alongside.

"Goodness, this is amazing," Milly commentated, joining Rose and Giles at their table.

"Very clever indeed," Giles agreed, clearly impressed. One could happily live in one of these touring the country, there's so much space…"
Each table had a glass bottle of tomato ketchup, vinegar, tartare sauce, salt and pepper. A small vase with a bright coloured daisy-type flower graced the centre of each table. Moola, Nazim and the children shared a table with Mr Pemberton.

"Right now, newspaper or plates?" Oliver called out?
Rose and Milly settled for plates. Giles and Mr Pemberton went for newspaper.

"Newspaper?" Moola and Nazim enquired quizzically.

"It's an old English tradition, fish and chips were always wrapped up in newspaper, no one bothered with plates," Mr Pemberton explained.

"Well, I think we will have ours in newspaper

please," said Nazim.

Mr Pemberton gave the family a big thumbs up.

"Tuck in everyone," Madge exclaimed as she gave everyone their food.

Mr Pemberton was taking pleasure in explaining all the various condiments on the table to a wide-eyed little Maryam. "My little girl Jennifer, used to love tomato sauce, had it with everything. Now, I am rather partial to tartare sauce..."

"Who wants tea?" Madge asked, brandishing, a huge, chrome teapot.

Everyone put their hands up.

"There's nothing like a cuppa with your fish and chips," she smiled as she filled everyone's cup.

As Milly sipped her tea, her, thoughts turned to Zoey and Richard. Milly was in on the secret. Richard was buying Zoey a puppy and had asked Milly permission to bring him or her back to the house briefly before they made their way home. Milly didn't need any persuading.

"Of course I don't mind, I love dogs. We had Rufus, a great big lolloping Great Dane for nearly fifteen years, he's buried in the garden... what are you getting?"

"A chocolate brown Labrador."

"Oh, lovely," Milly clapped her hands, "I can't wait to meet her."

"Do you think your other two guests are still on the beach Milly? Madge cut into Milly's reverie about the chocolate coloured puppy as she cleared the tables.

"Oh my goodness, Stephen and Gwen. Yes, I suppose they are."

"Not to worry," Oliver chipped in, "They can have theirs on the beach. It's a bit nippy out there so these should warm them up," he said, rolling up their fish and chips in an old copy of the Sunday Express.

Together they all trouped down to the sea. Milly couldn't recall the last time she'd been to the Witterings. *I really should come more often she mused, maybe I should get another dog.* They all walked on in companionable silence with little Maryam running on ahead.

"Baba! Mama!" she called, waving her arms excitedly, "Come, come…"

Moola collected up her skirts and ran after her daughter.

"Look, Mama! Look!"

Clearly distraught, Maryam pointed frantically to two stranded seals lying on the sea shore near her feet. One had a plastic bag over its face and was struggling to breathe. A couple of plastic cups were floating nearby with dead crabs floating inside. Nazim dropped to his knees and pulled the plastic off the first seal. It was lucky they found it then or it would surely have suffocated. After inhaling a large gulp of air it twitched its whiskers, gathered its strength and swam off. Maryam instinctively placed her small hands on the second seal which had bright orange, plastic netting wrapped tightly around its neck.

"Looks like it got caught in a torn fishing net," Nazim replied, anger etched on his face.

"We have to help it Baba," Maryam pleaded, as Moola looked on horrified.

"Do you have anything sharp in your bag?' Nazim asked Moola.

Moola searched in her bag but she knew she didn't have anything. As the others caught up, Nazim was gently untangling the mangled mess.

"Oh my goodness what's happened?" Rose asked, horrified. "Poor little thing…"

"Is it alive?" Milly gasped.

"Just," Giles said, placing a hand on its body.

"It is breathing but must be exhausted struggling to free itself!"

Everyone was transfixed as Nazim kept on unravelling the plastic netting. After what felt like an eternity he finally freed the seal from its captive hell. Instinctively everyone placed a comforting hand on its exhausted body and as they did so they felt an incredible healing heat emanate through their fingers.

"Mama my hands feel hot."

"Yes, mine too." Moola answered.

"It's healing energy, don't be afraid, it's good, I feel it too." Gwen interjected.

Everybody was experiencing the same sensation. Everybody was desperate in their own way for this innocent creature to survive the terrible insult inflicted upon it by mankind. It had to live. It had to breathe. All their problems seemed to dissipate in the presence of this little seal and its pain. Milly screwed up her eyes willing it to survive. Nazim, Mr Pemberton and Madge did the same.

"Breathe, please breathe," they all secretly chanted. *"Don't give up...*

Then, as if pulled back by an invisible force, they joined hands, making a protective circle around this beautiful, blameless, little creature; each person uttering their own prayer, willing it to live. Not to give up on life as they had all so nearly done in their own individual ways. *It must live. It had to live. Life was good. Life was a miracle. A gift.*

A series of gentle yet powerful waves rippled up towards the seal as they all gently doused it with the sea water. *Go, be free* Milly whispered, *Be free.*

They all cheered silently as it gasped for life with a shudder. It's beautiful, saucer-shaped eyes, fixed them with a stare as the gentle waves enveloped the creature. Nobody spoke.

Maryam's young, unblemished hand was protectively encased in Mr Pemberton's gnarled old one. Gwen instinctively took Milly's arm. Stephen watched silently as the creature was welcomed back into the sea. A hush descended on the group as they silently made their way back to the bus. Each one of them humbled beyond words by their shared experience on the beach.

***

There was a knock on the dining room door as Milly collected up the breakfast plates the next morning. It was Zoey, holding a wriggly, brown ball of fluff.

"Here she is," she beamed, "Meet Lulu."

"Oh Zoey, she is beautiful," Milly cooed stroking her gently.

"She just came straight over to me and demanded attention so we figured she was meant for us."

"Look how comfortable she is with you. She adores you."

Zoey beamed, holding the puppy closer.

"I think the lady said she had one who hadn't been homed." She looked at Milly with hopeful eyes. "They are based in Birdham."

"Yes, lovely little chap he was," Richard said as he came down the stairs with their cases. "We can just picture him here."

"I called the lady this morning and he's been ear-marked for someone else, but it looks like I'm getting a three-legged sausage dog-cross called Billy." Milly laughed, "He's not exactly what I envisaged but apparently he is very sweet and no one wants to adopt him, so I thought, 'he'll do'. They're bringing him round in a couple of days."

"How lovely, what a lucky little dog to end up with such a lovely home," Zoey beamed as Milly escorted them to their car.

"Thank you for a lovely stay," Richard, extended his hand. "We are so pleased we came. We've had a lovely Christmas."

"Yes, thank you Milly," Zoey chimed in. "We'd love to come back… With Lulu again, if that would be ok?"

"Of course, I'd love that... and you can meet Billy." *What a charming young couple they were with their fluffy little bundle.* Milly had to suppress a tear as their car crunched down the drive, bound for London town. But something told her they would be back.

James Pemberton was coming down the stairs with his suitcase as Milly went back into the house.

"Thank you, Milly, for such a wonderful Christmas, might I be able to say a quick goodbye to your charming Afghanistan family?"

"Of course, Mr Pemberton, take a seat in the dining room, I will go and give them a knock."

"Moola, Mr Pemberton is about to leave. Do you all have time to come down and say a quick goodbye?" Nazim poked his head out from their kitchenette.

"Of course, we will come down," he said, pulling on his jumper and giving his hair a quick comb.
Moola picked little Karim up from his cot and called Maryam, who promptly burst into tears when she heard that Mr Pemberton was going.

"We will miss you Sir," Nazim said extending his hand.

"And I will miss you. That's why I wanted to see you before I go. I would like you all to come and stay in my house one weekend. There's plenty of room and I have some lovely neighbours who I think would all love to meet you. I think they call it networking…"
Moola and Nazim smiled.

"So here is my card, give me a call a few days before you want to come and my housekeeper Jill, can get your rooms ready. You are always welcome."

"Thank you James, it was an honour to meet you."

"And it was a privilege to meet you and your beautiful family. Remember Nazim, that we all need a little help sometimes and I am here for you and your family."

"Thank you so much Sir," Nazim shook James' hand firmly. Thank you, that means so much."
Maryam slipped her hand into Mr Pemberton's as her father insisted on carrying James' case out to his car.

"Maybe you could sleep in my little girl, Jennifer's old room? She would like that."
Maryam nodded, tearfully.

"What does your mum think?" James smiled at Moola."

"I think Maryam would love that, Mr Pemberton."

***

Gwen was tapping away on her laptop in her room when there was a knock on her door. To her surprise she saw it was Stephen standing with his suitcase.

"Good morning Gwen, I just wanted to say a quick goodbye and thank you for our chat yesterday. Sometimes it's a lot easier to talk to a stranger."

"It is indeed and I am so glad we met," Gwen said extending her hand. "Are you off to your family now?"

"Yes," he looked at his feet, "I think it will be an extended stay."

"You will bounce back Stephen. You have your whole life ahead of you. This is just a blip."

"Yes, well, thank you Gwen."

"Thank you, Stephen, I don't know what I would have done without your calming presence yesterday when we discovered those poor creatures on the beach."

"I wish you'd let me drive you Mum," Giles said as he stood on the platform with Rose waiting for her train.

"I know it's against the rules but…"

"It is." Rose was firm. "I won't be there forever darling, things will work out."

"Yes, they will," Giles said emphatically. "They have to and soon. Remember you promised you would see a solicitor? I'm going to arrange that next week."

"Of course I will darling, how can I not, if you are kind enough to do that for me. It was a wonderful Christmas and so lovely to be back at 'Willow Cottage'."

"It was, we will go again."

"I'd like that."

There was a lump in Giles' throat as he watched his mother's train pull away.

A couple of stops before her train reached its destination, Rose saw she had a message from an unknown number on her phone.

Me mam sed can I stae wiv you on Nu Yars Eve coz she is goin owt.

A huge smile lit up Rose's face.

Of course you can Rory, I have missed you. Xxx

Madge came puffing down the stairs, followed by Oliver carrying their bags.

"Thank you for a splendid Christmas Milly, it was wonderful to spend time at 'Willow Cottage' again. We have so many wonderful memories here." Oliver held out his hand.

"We do indeed," Madge added.

"My pleasure, it wouldn't have been the same without our Pearly King and Queen and that fantastic bus trip, I've never had a more eventful Boxing Day."

"Yes that trip did rather bond us all... now then, a little bird told us you might be getting a dog? Holly always felt so much safer in the house with her dog Tess..."

"Well, now that my granddaughter Hope has heard all about my guest's getting a new puppy, she's talked me into getting its brother."

"Oh Milly," Madge squealed with delight, "How exciting, Oliver and I will have to come down and meet him."

"I'd like that," Milly replied, giving Madge an impromptu hug and waving them on their way.

The house felt incredibly empty now that the flamboyant Oliver and Madge had departed. Milly was tired but in a good way. It had been therapeutic for her to be so busy. And she was proud that the welcoming walls of 'Willow Cottage' had brought so many lonely people together this Christmas.

I did it Bill, and I think you would be proud of me.

As she sat nursing a coffee in the dining room, reflecting over her very different Christmas this year, her phone pinged with a message from Sophie.

Hey mum. How did everything go? I'm back next Thursday so thought I'd come and see you for a few days. Sorry we haven't managed to speak - my throat is hoarse with all this singing. I'm so happy Mum. I've found my singing voice again.

Next there was a message from her beloved grand-daughter, Hope.

Hey Nana, that's so cool that you went to the beach on Boxing Day in a London bus. Mum said she is coming to see you next Thursday so I thought I'd tag along too and maybe bring my boyfriend Toby? He's heard all about you and 'Willow Cottage'...

Thursday would be perfect darling. You can meet the newest member of our family.

OMG Nana, I've finally talked you round! You are getting a dog??

Yes, a sausage dog-cross with three legs!

Different... But typical you Nana. I'm buzzing XXX

There were other messages from Cy and Jake which Milly replied to. She was just tapping away when Gwen poked her head around the door, suitcase in hand.

"Oh Gwen, you are deserting me too."

"Yes, my darling, I think it's time you had some peace and quiet. Besides I will be back soon. Thank you for everything. By the way, I've got the title for my next book. – it's *'Christmas wishes at Willow Cottage."*

***

The End

Christmas wishes
from Chichester and beyond

"My Christmas wish is to send protective and healing wishes to the wonderful staff and patients at St Wilfrid's Hospice. A beautiful, peaceful sanctuary of endless love and giving."
Stephanie Lovelace
Supervisor, St Wilfrid's Hospice Charity Shop, Chichester

**

"We are grateful to be able to keep all our residents safe throughout the pandemic and now we are looking forward to Christmas when our residents can meet loved ones and make up for lost time."
Litia Badia,
Team Leader, Augusta Court, Care home, Chichester.

**

"Please can all the world leaders at the COP 26 conference in Glasgow 'Put their money where their mouth is'. They have to stop the ravages caused by climate change now. More action less talk. This is my Christmas wish."
Amy Owens
Mother of Malakai, 14, Hope, 10 and Jonny, 3. Sunbury

**

"My wish for Christmas is that our collective children do not worry or get overly stressed about catching up with their work after the disruption of Covid. Teachers and parents are there to support you. We can make up for lost time. We all get there in the end."
Mary McAveety, Teaching Assistant, St Mary's Catholic Primary School, Brook Green, London.

**

"The Salvation Army believe that every child should have a new toy at Christmas, this is made possible through our Xmas toy appeal. Merry Christmas to the children and people who donated toys. I would also like to pass seasonal greetings on to the wonderful staff at Portsmouth County Council who against all odds, managed to house so many of our homeless community both during Covid and this Christmas. God bless you all."

Tina Pink
Adherent at the Salvation Army community Centre, Portsmouth.

***

Acknowledgements

Whilst writing this book, I knew I needed to write a finale which brought all Milly's guests together in a dramatic way. Something had to happen to them collectively, as a group. Something they would never forget. Something that made them bond together even closer. A catalyst that proved just how precious and how wonderful life is and that we are all so lucky - just to be alive.
And then it came to me.
My ten-year-old, granddaughter told me about a film she had been shown at school. This was part of a writing exercise set for her class. It had a profound effect on her. She showed me the film on *YouTube* and I have to confess, it brought a tear to my eye. I knew Milly's guests were going to go on an unconventional bus trip to the beach on Boxing Day but what next? Then I remembered this film which gave me the idea of Milly and her guests finding a couple of stranded seals.

'Creature' has been written and directed by Tom Tagholm and produced by Park Pictures, an Academy Award-winning production company based in London, New York and Los Angeles.
It is a powerful film, with a powerful message.

A local community comes together to try and save a mysterious, marooned animal on the beach. For just over three minutes the film shows in heart-breaking detail how they desperately pull out a shocking assortment of plastic items from its body. The look on their faces says it all.

Launched by the environmental charity *Surfers Against Sewage* (SAS), these fantastic sea warriors are urging people in the UK to come together and sign its *#GenerationSea* petition urging the Prime Minister to introduce new laws and changes to save the seas and the creatures that live within them.

With 95% of the world's oceans still unexplored, the charity fears that without proper legal intervention, plastic pollution will continue to kill marine life that is yet to be discovered.

info@sas.org.uk
A grassroots movement that has grown into one of the UK's most active and successful environmental charities.

**

The poem on Rose's fridge was written by an unnamed, former resident at a women's refuge. All the women in that refuge have a copy of it in their rooms.

***

AFTERWORD

'Willow Cottage' is a seventeenth century ex-coaching inn, one-time school and brothel, which in its latest incarnation, my mother Sheila, ran very successfully as a 'Bed and Breakfast' establishment for thirty-odd years.

Many of the stories in the 'Willow Cottage Trilogy' are based on her experiences living and working in the house.

'Moving On', the last book in the trilogy, highlights the often unexpected, very close relationships that can exist between older and younger people, as well as the pain of coming to terms with Dementia and how that can impact on the emotional and financial stability of a family.

We had hoped that Sheila could have spent her last days in 'Willow Cottage' but sadly, this wasn't meant to be.

I am however, happy to say that 'Willow Cottage' wasn't bought by a developer and turned into characterless, money-making apartments. It is still a family house and a delightful young family are now the new custodians of 'Willow Cottage.'

We hope they enjoy as many happy years there as we did.

Clare Cassy

The Willow Cottage Trilogy
Book One:

The Bed & Breakfast Queen
by
Clare Cassy

The Willow Cottage Series begins with Holly Bradbury, a disillusioned 30-something writer, questioning the life she has made for herself with her partner in their busy, so-called glamorous careers in publishing and advertising.

When an opportunity to change her life presents itself in the form of an advert for 'Willow Cottage', Holly jumps in feet first to become a 'Bed and Breakfast Queen.'

Read about her adventures with unpredictable guests, an eccentric cleaning lady, a massive dog and an exciting stranger, as she discovers being a 'Bed and Breakfast Queen' can be frustrating, moving and sometimes just plain hilarious.

***

The Willow Cottage Trilogy
Book Two:

Sunny Side Up
by
Clare Cassy

Milly Henderson has just turned sixty.
While her friends mark retirement with the obligatory
world cruise, Milly's golden years look set to lose their
sheen.
Her dream of putting her feet up and retiring to sunnier
climes has been snatched away and she finds herself
having to think about making a living for the first time in
forty years.
Running a 'B&B' is the perfect answer.
She can live where she works and work where she lives.
But never knowing who you are inviting into your house is
a worry and along with a resident ghost and gift of a pet
pig, Milly has to contend with a whole host of colourful
and often unpredictable guests.

***

The Willow Cottage Trilogy
Book Three:

Moving On
by
Clare Cassy

Milly Henderson has run the renowned 'Willow Cottage' B&B for twenty odd years. Now eighty and a 'not so merry widow', Milly is tired and wants to hand over the reins of her precious B&B to her daughter, Sophie.

Sophie is a financially squeezed, emotionally-challenged, single mum, living in London with a wayward teenager and flagging career. Her sensible head tells her to make the move but her much-loved mother's increasingly erratic behaviour is a worry.
What happens if they fall out - or her daughter absconds back to London?

It's a big decision.

***

BED & BREAKFAST
QUEEN

CLARE CASSY

'An Excerpt from The Bed and Breakfast Queen'.

"What? You're going to give everything up to run a Bed and Breakfast in the back of beyond? You can't be serious?" Mac scoffed, as Holly was stirring a bolognaise sauce that evening. "You're clearly in line to be editor Hol. You must be mad... Burying yourself in the country, slaving over a pan of bacon and eggs... tripping over bundles of dirty washing!"

Holly sighed. She was losing him. His body language said it all. At one time, he would have his arms around her waist, nuzzling her neck as she was cooking. But now he was coming home later and later from the office.

"I'm tired of chasing scummy stories and persuading people to sell their souls for a few hundred quid Mac... Yes, it's been fun and I love everybody I work with on the magazine, but I am tired. I've done it since I was nineteen and now I've turned thirty, I want to do something else. It's a fantastic property, at a knock down price, it could be a new start for us both."

Holly looked at him with hope in her eyes as she re-filled their wine glasses.

"Just come and see it with me. Please Mac?"

Mac pushed his thick mop of blond hair back from his face as he went through the motions of looking at the property details Holly had laid out on their stainless-steel kitchen worktop.

It was obvious he wasn't interested in going to see it with her. Holly sighed sadly as she turned her attention to serving their food. They ate in silence. An awkward, heavy presence hanging in the air.

Both worked hard and were successful in their respective careers. He was Creative Director of one of the most successful advertising agencies in London, while Holly was Features Editor for a well-known women's weekly magazine. They went away for week-ends to Paris, Florence, Barcelona and Rome, ate at the best restaurants. Drank in all the well-known media drinking bars. Life had been good until Holly accidently became pregnant.

It was a shock to them both as she'd been having regular contraceptive injections for the past three years and had never missed an appointment for a top-up treatment. Until last month. Mac was furious and blamed her for their predicament.

"How could you have been so irresponsible?" he'd shouted at her, that awful night in the restaurant. "Didn't you note down the date of your appointment? How the hell could you have missed it?"

"I had a deadline Mac, and couldn't leave the office. Work took over and I just forgot to go. I didn't do it on purpose if that's what you are thinking."

"I don't know what to think," he'd hissed at her. The sad thing was that she'd been so excited when the line turned blue on the pregnancy test and was sure he would come around; after all it wasn't as if they were in the first flush of youth, they were financially secure – living in Mac's spacious, ultra-modern, high tech apartment in London's fashionable East End and had been together for five good years.

"Things worked out for Abigail and Pete," Holly added in a softer tone. "Look how devastated he was when she told him she was pregnant."

"True, now he's an even bigger baby bore than she is. Don't you remember that awful night we went out with them and all they talked about was liquidising baby food? I'm sorry Holly, I'm just not ready to be a father." Avoiding her eyes and fiddling nervously with the cutlery in front of him, it was clear that the subject wasn't up for further discussion.

"So, I'm good enough to sleep with for five years but not good enough to have your child... is that it?" She was starting to shout and Mac was looking mortified as the couple on the next table were clearly ear-wigging.

"If this child was the result of a one night stand I could understand Mac."
Unable to bear his callous attitude any longer, her eyes had filled with tears as she flung down her napkin, marched out the restaurant and hailed a cab home.

"You alright luv?" The kindly cabbie had asked.

"Yes, fine thanks," she stammered, choking back huge, thick sobs that strangled her voice. Then to her amazement she told him everything.

"Don't worry, he'll come 'round luv, that's men for ya. See these?..." he said, proudly pointing out five or six pictures of children of various ages pinned around the inside of his cab, "They're me pride and joy, all five of 'em. But when the missus told me she was first expectin' I thought me world 'ad come to an end. You'll see luv, he'll come 'round. Five years you've been together? Course 'e will..."

But Mac didn't. When he came back later that night they slept as far apart from each other as they could. He undressed in silence as Holly sobbed into the sheets. The silence between them was deafening and two weeks later, she had a miscarriage. Mac was foul and his distant and uncaring attitude to her distress was proving to be the death knoll for their relationship.
But someone or something, was tweaking Holly's destiny.

She was recovering at home when her mother rang.

"Holly darling, I have a letter for you. Looks like it is from Auntie Maud. Shall I forward it, or will you get it when you come down?" she asked hopefully.
Holly wasn't in the best frame of mind to visit her parents. She was so miserable she could hardly bear her own company let alone be around anyone else.

"Do you mind reading it to me Mum?"
There was a rustle of paper as her mother opened the letter.

"God... her writing. I can barely read it... right..."
Holly's mother took a deep breath.

Dearest, darling Holly,
I don't think I have long for this world. Don't be sad, I have spent too long on this earth.

"Oh, my goodness," Holly's mum gulped...
I would like you to buy yourself a house with whatever is left of my estate once the nursing home where I have resided these last few years has been paid. Your mother and father worry about you, as do I.

*Get out of London dear. Buy yourself a house in a proper
part of England. Somewhere where the air is fresh and you
can find yourself a good man, who will love and cherish
you and your children. Don't leave it too late like your old
Auntie Maud.*
I have instructed my solicitor accordingly.

Your loving,
Great Auntie Maud

"Oh my God Mum!" Holly burst into tears.

"Dear, Oh, dearie me," her mother repeated in
between sobs. It was a full five minutes before either of
them could draw breath. It was as if the old lady knew
what had happened between Holly and Mac.
But she couldn't possibly have known, because Holly
hadn't even told her mother about her miscarriage.

The day after they received her letter, Auntie Maud
died a spinster. Colin, her childhood sweetheart, who she
called out for on her deathbed, was killed in the Second
World War. Shot down with his crew in their Lancaster
bomber, somewhere over Germany. He'd just turned
eighteen and was the rear gunner. He'd lied about his age
to join the Air Force.

"No one could match Colin," Auntie Maud would say,
adding wistfully, "Besides, after the war there weren't
enough men left to go around. I wasn't the only girl never
to get married. There was a whole bunch of us."
So she ended her days in a nursing home in Eastbourne
after a life looking after other people's children. Holly had
many happy memories of spending time with her. Looking
at faded old photos of Colin; baking or sewing in her
house which smelt of cats and mothballs.

"Auntie Maud would have been a wonderful mother,"
Holly's mother used to say, "She just had that way with
children."

She gave Holly the letter at the old lady's funeral and

Holly re-read the feminine, spidery handwriting at her graveside.

"Thank you, Auntie Maud," she whispered, placing Colin's photo and a bouquet of violets - her auntie's favourite flowers, on her grave. She could picture her in her bed at the nursing home; propped up like a little bird in her nest of white pillows; clad in a pink, winceyette nightie, her long, thin, grey hair neatly styled into a bun at the nape of her neck. The faded photograph of her beloved Colin, on her bedside table. Life could be so cruel, Holly reflected sadly; so many of Auntie Maud's generation were denied the chance of marriage and a normal, family life, as were a lot of women in Holly's generation now; albeit in a different way because Holly wasn't the only one of her friends itching to hang up her corporate suit and have a baby. Then, when and if they became a mother, they had to rush back to work to pay the mortgage with constant feelings of guilt that they couldn't spend more time at home. Women like her friend Maggie, who was dreading going back to the job she hated after the birth of her baby, but had no choice. Maggie's husband had also made it very clear that they could never afford to have another child either.

"I'd have loved to have had more children," Maggie had said, wistfully, adding: "What I'd do to stay at home and make playdoh and jam tarts."

In many ways, Holly's mother and her generation who married and had children in the 1950's didn't know how lucky they were. As much as Mum moaned about having to be a 'stay-at-home mother,' she never battled with the exhaustion and guilt that so many of Holly's generation of young working mothers faced every day.

Maybe the old lady was right and Holly would be happier in a 'Proper part of England,' the idea of moving out of London and finding a husband who could cherish her and their baby would be wonderful.

Yes, Auntie Maud, I am going to leave London and start a new life, somewhere where the air is fresh and clean...
Rest in peace, with your Colin.

Holly was just reading the cards on the flowers when her mother came hobbling over in her high heels, dramatically holding on to her hat.

"Holly darling, there you are. We're making our way to the hotel for drinks. Dad's just getting the car," she said, getting all motherly and linking arms with her only daughter. "You are looking a bit peaky dear."

"I'm alright." Holly lied.

"Good, now you must talk to your cousin Grace. Did I tell you she's pregnant? My sister's going to be a grandmother! I always thought it would be me first." she sighed, holding tighter on to Holly's arm.

***

'You have reached your destination.'
Thank God for my Sat Nav, Holly mused as she saw the impressive iron, black and white Bed and Breakfast sign gently swaying in the West Sussex wind. She'd never been any good at reading maps and was sure she wouldn't have found her way without it.

Indicating right as directed, she drove slowly down the long, sweeping, tree-lined driveway into the '*Willow Cottage Bed and Breakfast*' establishment. Her car tyres slowly crunching over the pearl-grey coloured gravel. Then, carefully parking her pink Volkswagen Beetle and switching off the engine, she checked her hair in the car's mirror, put a dab of powder on her nose and renewed her trade-mark, cherry red lipstick. Not bad timing; she'd driven down from London in just over an hour and a half and was five minutes early for her appointment with Mrs Baxter, the vendor.

The word 'Cottage' was misleading, to say the least, as there were sixteen bedrooms. Built in a classic Elizabethan 'L' shape, it was painted an attractive shade of green. Roses clustered around the door way and Hollyhocks and Delphiniums vied for attention with Lilac, Marigolds, Daisies and Sweet Peas in the long front garden.

How clean the air smelt after London, the sky was a bright blue and Holly could swear she hadn't seen such white, fluffy clouds in a very long time. Two sweet, little robins were pecking excitedly at some breadcrumbs scattered on a windowsill.

Holly's high heels sank into the gravel as she made her way down the side of the house to the front entrance.

A massive dog with a very loud, deep bark bounded to the front door as soon as she rang the bell. A moment or so later, it was answered by a small, fresh faced woman carrying a chunky baby. She looked around thirty, the same age as Holly, with unkempt, shoulder length hair. As her eyes scanned Holly, her face dropped. Somehow, she couldn't see such a 'girl about town' in her pencil skirt and tasteful silk blouse turning out plates of eggs and bacon every morning.

Christine Baxter sighed to herself as she invited her in. She was bound to be another time waster, traipsing through the house making infuriating comments about all the improvements she would make.

"Miss Bradbury?"

"Yes, that's me," Holly answered brightly.

"And you must be Mrs Baxter?"

"I am. And this is Tess," she said wearily, indicating the dog, to assure Holly it wouldn't eat her for breakfast.

"Her bark is a lot worse than her bite, don't worry."

Thank God for that, thought Holly. She liked dogs but this one was huge – an English Bullmastiff apparently, and she wouldn't want to get on the wrong side of it.

"Your baby is lovely, how old is he?... She?"

"He. Bobby, five months." Mrs Baxter answered proudly, jiggling him on her hip. He was so perfect with his little rosebud mouth and shock of dark hair. Holly's breath was momentarily taken away as she felt a surge of longing, crossed with a familiar, stabbing loss.

What would our baby have looked like at this age?

She would have liked to have held little Bobby but Mrs Baxter kept him protectively tucked under her ample arm.

Tapestries and pictures of various country scenes adorned the walls of the entrance hall. A small table by the front-door was crowded with business cards and tourist guides of every shape and size. Following Mrs Baxter, baby and dog, Holly made her way past a large kitchen and laundry room into a spacious back sitting room with a very attractive, open brick fireplace.

"Sit yourself down," Mrs Baxter gestured politely, indicating the sofa, the majority of which was immediately swiped by the dog. "Don't mind Tess, she's an asset in a place like this, you never know who is going to turn up at your door."

Still cradling her baby, she explained that they lived in this part of the house while the rest of the property was set-aside for guests. A small bathroom and a box-room for the baby led off from the sitting room, while the Baxters' bedroom and adjoining store-room were more modern additions to the house. Holly had the feeling this wasn't going to be a very long tour of the house. Mrs Baxter seemed tired and was obviously pre-occupied with the baby.

Where was her husband? Shouldn't he be showing her around as the poor woman was obviously so exhausted? Holly was dying for a coffee but she didn't really blame Mrs Baxter for not offering her one. It couldn't be much fun having people tramp through your house especially when it was so large and you had to lug a chunky baby around.

The kitchen was a million miles from the high-tech minimalist, chrome one Holly and Mac shared in London. Holly loved the long, scrubbed, pine trestle table and matching impressive dresser, cluttered with brightly coloured china.

A welcoming warmth and smell of baking emanated from the Aga cooker as Mrs Baxter led Holly through to the dining-room. About half a dozen little tables sporting yellow and white checked table cloths were covered with an assortment of stainless-steel teapots and little jugs.

The table cloths would have to go, they must be white linen, Holly mused.

Used, individual tubs of butter, marmalade and jam were piled in pyramids on empty plates.

"Haven't had a chance to clear up yet what with the little one and all." Mrs Baxter apologised with a soft Sussex burr.

The dining room also had a large open fireplace complete with brass bellows, pokers and decorative, iron kettles. An attractive arrangement of dried hops and various brass pans and iron ornaments hung on the walls and a nicely worn Persian carpet added a bit of colour and style to the practical beige carpet.

Nice rug but the carpet's worn and grimy...

"My guests tell me what time they want breakfast the night before and if they want a 'Full English.' Boiled eggs are the worst," Mrs Baxter smiled. "Some want 'em soft, others 'ard. People gets very fussy about their eggs."

Baby Bobby's eyes studied Holly's face over his mother's shoulder as they left the dining room and mounted the wonderful, sweeping staircase with its wide, shiny, mahogany banister to the bedrooms. *There'd be no need for Pilates classes after a daily workout like this.* Suddenly, Mrs Baxter stopped in her tracks and doubled back to a room she had seemingly forgotten.

"Now this be the Dame School," she said, as they stepped into a huge musty smelling room cluttered with stepladders and old paint pots. Apparently, it had been added to the house in the latter part of the eighteen hundreds.

"Them that could afford it, paid a penny a week to 'ave their kiddies learn to read and write and there be the picture to prove it," Mrs Baxter gushed, pointing to a faded old photograph hanging perilously on the wall by a rusty nail.

"That there, be the dame, their teacher, a Miss Gibbons I'm told."

Spellbound, Holly studied the faces of the ragged looking

little Victorian children, standing to attention next to the fierce old woman who was clad entirely in black, save for her white bonnet.

"Buried in the churchyard, she is… and probably along with some of them little nippers as well." Reluctantly, Holly tore herself away from the picture as Mrs Baxter called her over to a door, which opened out to an outside staircase. Its crumbling, moss-covered, steps descending right down to the back garden.

"See that there oak tree? The family that owned this 'ouse hid King Charles in it when he was fleeing from them Roundheads…"

How could Mrs Baxter bear to leave this house? It was wonderful.

The baby was starting to get a bit tetchy and Holly sensed his mother wanted to get the rest of the viewing over. The bedrooms on the next two floors were named after flowers. There was the pink 'Foxglove' room, the blue 'Delphinium', white 'Heliotrope' and the mauve 'Lilac Room.' And that was just for starters. Holly's favourite was the yellow 'Primrose Room' at the top of the house with its sloping ceiling, charming window seat and pretty, stained-glass window.

Um, maybe that could be mine… All had their own little sinks, television and tea and coffee making facilities.

I'll have to invest in new bed linen, Holly mused. People don't like sleeping in flowery bed sheets any more. It had to be white, crisp Egyptian cotton… and the televisions looked a bit old fashioned as well. Everyone expected flat screen, wall mounted TVs now.

"Now this be our Honeymoon suite," Mrs Baxter laughed, a twinkle in her eye, as they walked up to the third floor.

"It's lovely." Holly remarked truthfully, eyeing the Victorian style cherub above the huge four-poster bed and nicely faded tapestries adorning the walls.

"You have to watch wedding parties tho," Mrs Baxter added. "They can get a bit boisterous sometimes! The last lot smashed all me champagne glasses. Nice little money earners tho'... right, I'll show you the Brewery next," she said, shifting baby Bobby on her hip.

"Oh, that sounds interesting." Holly said brightly, following her gingerly, down a perilous, creaky little back staircase.

The Brewery, Mrs Baxter explained, was the oldest part of the house. It had originally been a coaching inn and this was where the horses were rested and beer was served to passing travellers. An attractive modern-day mural of Tudor wenches pouring beer inside a rowdy inn, with boys brushing horses and feeding dogs outside, was painted on one of the walls in the little entrance hall...

"My friend's daughter, painted that when she was fresh out of art school." Mrs Baxter said proudly.
It was exquisite.

Holly was enthralled as Mrs. Baxter pulled back the corner of an old Persian rug revealing a rusty metal plate embedded in the floor.

"There's a secret tunnel under 'ere," she said, tapping it with her foot, "Goes straight out to Fishbourne Creek it does... used by boot-leggin pirates doin' their business right 'ere in this brewery with the inn-keeper."

"Oh my god, have you been down there?"

"My hubby tried. Was a helluva job getting this lid off, but the 'ole had all closed up... 'e did a bit a diggin' - mess everywhere there was, but he soon gave up."

Holly could just picture a bunch of rag-tag, Johnny Depp look-alike, pirates jumping up and out of the tunnel. They probably stood right where she and Mrs Baxter were now. All wiping sweaty brows after the exertions of rolling and heaving up heavy barrels of booze. Candles would be flickering, a tiny mouse scampering here and there along the dusty, flag stones on the brewery floor. The atmosphere would be tense as the inn keeper inspected the barrels. Then after greedily gulping a beer they'd count the coins they'd been given and beat a hasty retreat down the tunnel to their boats in the harbour.

This house was steeped in history. Holly had never bought a property before but she knew she wanted this one. It had a warm, almost humbling presence and she knew she could be at home here. Forcing herself to go, she thanked Mrs Baxter for her time and said she'd contact the agent to make an offer.

Mrs Baxter didn't look convinced.

"Mac, the house has so much potential. It's all beams and creaky staircases, the bedrooms need updating but with a few changes here and there, it could be a gold mine. There's even a secret tunnel running out to Fishbourne Creek. No wonder it's a favourite with the Americans… You'll love it. Let's talk tonight, I'll be back around seven. Just going to do a little shopping in Chichester…"

***

Continued in 'The Bed and Breakfast Queen'.

Available at Amazon.co.uk

Also by Clare Cassy

TWO OF A KIND

How many chances does one person have to find true love? When Juanita Estevez' path crosses with Santi Alverez, a world-famous fashion photographer who rudely snaps a picture of her when she is out shopping, their worlds are turned upside down as they come to realise that they are 'Two of a Kind'. Both fiercely ambitious, passionate and supremely talented at what they do. But having a talent often has its price.

Can they ever be together and if so, how?

***

All Titles available as an eBook or Paperback on Amazon.co.uk

Audio books coming soon.

Look out for the latest book by Clare Cassy
Coming soon in 2022

'Bunking In'

Stylish, seventy-something Silvia rattles around in a huge house she can't bear to sell. Cecily, one of her oldest and dearest friends has fallen on hard times. Unhappy where she lives, Silvia suggests she moves in and they grow old together disgracefully.

To Cecily's dismay, Silvia then takes in a family of Syrian refugees. Not the best mother in the past, Silvia is happy to have another crack at honing her mothering skills. While childless, plain and sensible Cecily has a taste of motherhood. Having new young blood around gives them both a renewed zest for life.

Then little Ali and his father leave. Can these two adoring, substitute mums, resurrect the remaining brother's dreams?

**

Printed in Great Britain
by Amazon